"I've always been honest.

"All these years, I've warned you to stay away, so if I tell you that you can trust me then you should believe me, right?"

"I guess so." Juniper studied her nails.

"I promise to finish the renovations before I return to work and that I won't run off without a word. And you promise to relax a little." Hudson offered his hand.

"Fine, I agree." She shook his hand but withdrew before he could register her touch.

He didn't like it. She'd always pursued him, and he'd always been the one to pull away. Not that it mattered; nothing had changed. Juniper deserved a good man in her life and so did Gracie. They needed a man who would be soft-spoken, generous and kind. Hudson knew how to take what he wanted, make money and work hard. Not good qualities for a husband or father.

The turn to the long drive didn't come soon enough, because the longer he sat in the car with Juniper, the more his imagination took him on a drive into what-if land.

Ciara Knight, a *USA TODAY* bestselling and award-winning author, is known for her "Southern Grace to Western Embrace" stories. She has captivated over a million readers with over fifty novels, exploring heartwarming and inspirational romance from Southern landscapes to the West. Inspired by her husband, children and dream of sailing the world, Ciara invites you to visit ciaraknight.com for news, booklists and adventures.

Books by Ciara Knight

Love Inspired

A Blessing in Disguise

Visit the Author Profile page at LoveInspired.com.

A BLESSING IN DISGUISE

CIARA KNIGHT

ISBN-13: 978-1-335-93186-3

A Blessing in Disguise

For questions and comments about the quality of this book, please contact us at CustomerService@Harlequin.com.

® is a trademark of Harlequin Enterprises ULC.

Love Inspired
22 Adelaide St. West, 41st Floor
Toronto, Ontario M5H 4E3, Canada
www.LoveInspired.com

Printed in U.S.A.

And we know that all things work together for good to them that love God, to them who are the called according to his purpose.

—*Romans* 8:28

To God's greatest blessings in my life—my family.
You are my inspiration and my heart.

Chapter One

Atlanta's gridlock traffic broke free, giving way to shrinking buildings, tall pines and Hudson Kenmore's complicated past. A past he'd spent fifteen years avoiding in his rearview mirror, only to drive head-on at the memories now.

At the Willow Oaks exit the road dipped down, leaving his stomach behind—or maybe that was guilt steeling his resolve. How could he face the woman who'd practically raised him, after abandoning her for fifteen years to make his own way in life? How could he say no when she called and asked for help? He owed her so much—a week of a few chores and good food would be a small price to pay for all she'd done for him over the years. She'd been his sanctuary, offering faith and fun away from his own home full of sadness. Besides, now that his company had closed the multimillion-dollar resort deal in the Caribbean, he could take a short break from work and let his partner rest and recuperate from his chemo.

He hung a left at the end of the ramp. Nothing

but trees and bugs and gossip around for miles. Town gossip that could spin a tale faster than a tornado could suck up and spit out a trailer.

Downtown Willow Oaks came into view. Potted plants hung from faux gas lampposts, striped awnings stretched from two-story redbrick buildings and people wandered about as if time moved slower. A world away, but only forty or so miles south of Atlanta.

To his surprise, some of the storefronts stood empty with cracked windows taped up, while a scattering of familiar shops remained, and still others were new. A Realtor, barber, hardware store, inn, feedstore, and a fishing and hunting shop lined the right side of the road. A craft place, grocery, hair salon and café to the left. At the corner, he spotted the florist and knew he couldn't show up empty-handed. Not to see his grandmother who'd taught him never to arrive at a lady's house without a gift in hand. The woman was all faith and no drama. He didn't understand it, but he admired it.

It had only taken two minutes of a phone conversation for him to agree to help with any repairs and to even muck the stalls as penance for not coming to see her sooner. That and his partner manipulating him with his so-called dying wish. The man would beat cancer and conquer the world at the same time.

Orange cones and construction tape around a massive pothole blocked the parking lot, so he swung around and parked on Main Street in front of Bless Your Heart Café.

He shoved the car into Park and stepped out to unfurl his long legs and straighten his spine, which ached from sitting all day on a plane and then in the car.

"Hey, there." A hunched man with gray hair and big teeth stood at the curb. Hudson feared the man would fall if he stepped down from the sidewalk, so he hurried to his side and guided the elder away from the road.

"You going to the café?" the man asked.

"Nope. Just stopping to pick something up."

Hudson eyed the man with the thick, black-rimmed glasses and thought he looked familiar, but after fifteen years, people changed.

The man slid his glasses to the end of his nose and peered over the rims. "Right, sorry for your loss."

"My loss?" Hudson shoved his keys into his pocket and took the man by the elbow to lead him to a bench so he could sit down before his shaking legs gave way.

A young girl ran over. "Papa, this way." She took her grandfather's hand and guided him to another car.

Poor grandpa obviously suffered from dementia. Hudson strolled up the sidewalk breathing in the fresh country air and enjoying the sun on his face. This time of year was beautiful.

He sneezed.

Beautiful scenery with deadly pollen. He'd forgotten that part and made a mental note to pick up some allergy meds if Nana didn't have any.

People stared at him from a bench out front of the barbershop, pointing and whispering. Obviously, the breeze still carried the news around town, the hot whispering wind of the people sharing the latest and greatest gossip. Yep, he'd expected some locals would be spinning tales of why he'd left for so long.

Hudson rounded the corner and yanked the rough metal handle on the glass door, causing a bell to jingle over his head. He stepped inside the florist shop, bombarded by a floral scent that made his eyes water. "Good afternoon. I'm here to pick up some flowers for my grandmother."

"Aren't you a little late?" the young woman with blue hair asked from behind the counter. Apparently, even the young folk knew he'd taken fifteen years to return. His gut clenched tight with guilt, but he wouldn't run from it any longer and he wouldn't engage in idle gossip or defend his life choices to a woman with an interesting fashion sense. Instead, he reached for the tulips in the potted plant. His grandmother loved tulips and hated waste, so they looked perfect.

The woman with the tilted name tag that read Mindi on her blue vest raised her pierced eyebrow at him. "Ah, those are Juniper's favorite."

That was a name he hadn't heard in a long time. Hudson wondered how this woman knew Juniper, since she'd moved away after she married, but he ignored the girl's comment, paid her and left the store.

Juniper Keller, his childhood friend with pigtails who'd mucked the stalls and worked with her father on his grandmother's farm, who followed Hudson to the swimming hole and the barn and the house and everywhere he'd tried to hide from her. Despite only having a one-year age difference, he'd never allowed himself to think of her as more than a friend. Not until they were older, and even then he denied his feelings because she was his everything. Until that one day he kissed her. The day that forced him to face the fact that he needed to leave because he'd never be good enough for her. And when she grew up and appeared unannounced at his dorm to win him over with a declaration of her love, he'd done the right thing for her—set her up with his roommate, knowing she'd be better off with any man other than himself.

If he was honest, Juniper had grown up pretty,

but his mother had been a sweet, small-town girl whom his dad had manipulated and driven into an early grave. Nope. He would've done the same to sweet, naive little Juniper Keller. She was all sunshine and rainbows, and he was dark clouds and storms.

To his relief, he managed to slip into his car without further interaction. He headed out the other side of town, passed the cornfield, the old cotton field, the abandoned mill, and hung a right onto the dirt road leading deep, deep, deeper into the property at the edge of the county.

The trees opened to the old farmhouse on the hill with the green tin roof and white front porch. A tickle of anticipation surprised him.

But only a few cows grazed in the front pasture and the grass stood tall, too tall. It would invite snakes into the farm.

He rounded the final turn on the long drive and noticed no dogs chased his rental car. Perhaps they were being fed. Strange time of day to be doing that from what he remembered.

Wood slats leaned against the walls of the barn, leaving gaping holes for animals to scurry in and out of, and the chicken coop wire was bent and broken.

Still, the farm offered open land, pretty scenery and no internet. Hudson wasn't sure if he was in paradise or purgatory.

Excitement welled up inside him, and he realized how much he'd missed Nana. He parked in front of the house, hurried from the car, and inhaled the smell of horse and dirt and cow patties. He'd forgotten that part.

With flowers in hand, he bolted up the evergreen steps to the screen door and wrenched it open with a loud squawk. He turned the knob and shoved the front door, but it didn't open. Since when did Nana start locking up during the day?

He saddled the pot of tulips on his hip and knocked. "Hey, Nana, it's me."

Footsteps sounded, the lock clicked and the door swung open, but Nana didn't stand there. Juniper Keller—a not-so-young-and-awkward, grown-up version—met his eyes.

"Ah, hi. I didn't know you'd be here," he mumbled like a second grader on a playground date, kicking himself for stumbling back into childish stammering he'd thought long gone.

"What're you doing here?" Juniper stood rod straight with a narrow-eyed gaze and a snippy tone. Nothing like the sweet girl he remembered.

Agitation pricked him. "I'm here to see my grandmother. I didn't expect to see you and James here."

She huffed with all the attitude of a big-city girl and none of her previous sweet, country charm. Things had definitely changed. "You won't," she said before she pushed the door to shut it, as if to dismiss him from his own grandmother's home.

He stuck his foot between the door and the frame. "Won't what?"

"See James here. We're divorced."

A jolt of relief bolted through him, leaving confusion in its wake. He cleared his throat and fought to find the right words. He might not want to marry Juniper, but any sane man without baggage couldn't deny her beauty. "I'm sorry to hear that." He stepped forward but she pressed a hand to his chest.

"What are you doing?"

"Coming inside to see my grandmother."

"You're too late."

He eyed his watch. "Atlanta traffic, you know, but she's expecting me."

Juniper shook her head and let out a nervous chuckle. "A day too late. Her funeral was yesterday."

Juniper fought the panic sending her heart into her throat. The man she'd loved all her life, the man she'd tried to win over through more than one rejection, had probably arrived now to kick her out of the only home she'd ever known. She had no choice but to let him in, though.

This house belonged to him.

She stepped back and made her way to the living room to sit on the 1800s antique chair before her legs collapsed.

"I don't understand. I just spoke to her." Hudson entered the room and eyed the place as if it had changed beyond his recognition, but nothing had been moved or altered for two generations. He set the pot of tulips on the side table and removed his tailor-made jacket. The man stood tall and strong and distractingly handsome as always.

"She passed away three days ago." Juniper kept her head high and faced the man who held her and her daughter's fate in his hands. A man who didn't know how to be kind or selfless. She said a silent prayer for guidance.

"Why didn't someone contact me?" He looked lost and confused. As if he couldn't process the news. If it had been anyone else, Juniper would've broken the news slowly and gently, but Hudson had said long ago not to waste his time with feelings. He lived with facts, not emotions.

"I called your office."

Hudson paced around the old sage couch with wood accents and the walnut wood table, and collapsed on the wingback armchair. "I wasn't at my office."

"Despite the fact that you made it plain long ago you didn't want me in your life, I tried to call you, but your secretary would never put me through. I left messages and figured she'd give them to you. And I couldn't find your cell number in Nana's address book." The clock on the wall chimed two, warning Juniper that Gracie would be waking from her nap soon.

Juniper needed to figure out how to get Hudson to let her remain in the home until he probably auctioned it off to the highest bidder. That would buy her some time to straighten out her life. Even better if she could convince Hudson to keep the place and allow her to start the business she'd planned to run with Nana Kenmore.

"My secretary left on maternity leave." Hudson rubbed his forehead as if the news still hadn't sunk in. "What are you doing here?"

Juniper pointed at the hospital bed in the next room where the dining table used to be. "I've been taking care of your grandmother the last year since she began having trouble keeping up with things on her own. She's been kind, and we've enjoyed working together."

"I didn't know." Hudson dropped his hands to his thighs, his gaze downcast and his shoulders slumped.

"Now you do." Her chest tightened and she longed to reach for him, to soothe his pain. She'd never seen Hudson anything but stoic and proud. Emotions had never played a part in his world except for when he'd laughed at one of her jokes or splashed at the swimming hole when they were kids. Nana Kenmore had always said that Juniper brought out the best in Hudson. Too bad he'd brought out the worst in her.

He scrubbed his face clean of emotion and pushed from the couch. "Okay, so I need to take care of things then. Where's her will? Is she buried at the family plot?" His rushed words tumbled out of his mouth faster than his feet paced the small space. "And I need her account information and the deed to this place."

It didn't take long for the Hudson Kenmore she knew to show up, front and center. His words spun like an EF5 tornado blasting her with questions. "Always about business, isn't it? That's how you deal with life. You hide behind work." Where would she go? How would she care for her daughter?

He stopped dead and faced her, blinking with a confused eyebrow raise.

Juniper prayed for calm, but she should've prayed longer because she stood and blocked his path to the study. "You have no right. You've been gone forever, and this is my home now. I can't leave. I don't have anywhere else to go."

"You don't have any savings?" Hudson asked in a shocked tone.

"I have savings, but it's more complicated than that."

"What's the complication?"

Juniper realized she had to slow this conversation down and think of how to handle this better. She needed to take notes from the Hudson Handbook on Business Dealings. She inhaled a deep breath and forced a calm to her voice. "Let's take a step back and start over. We're both emotional right now. I'll pour us some tea and we can have a proper conversation."

"That's what Nana would do." He nodded his agreement and picked up an old picture of the four of them on the farm. He looked lost and alone. "Where's your father?"

"He died five years ago." Juniper went to the kitchen and leaned against the island. She rubbed her chest where that tightness had settled the day that Nana had passed away. First her father died, then her divorce, then Nana. Too much loss in too short a time. No one would help her make a life here, so she needed to convince Hudson she could do this on her own.

She closed her eyes and thought about how to convince Hudson not to sell the place and to instead allow her to start an equestrian program for people with physical and developmental challenges. He was all business, so she'd start with facts and end with statistics.

She pulled the pitcher of tea from the refrigerator and poured two glasses, then returned to the living room.

The afternoon sunlight flooded in, heating the room. Hudson stood looking out the window. He held Nana's Bible in his hands. A Bible passed down from her grandmother. A Bible Juniper knew Nana would want Hudson to have. "Please, sit. I have a business proposition for you. Hear me out, and then I'll produce all the documents you've asked for."

He offered a curt nod and sat across the table from her. She could tell he wore his business persona to mask his broken heart. "I'll listen."

"When I returned here, I didn't have anyone. You know my mother died when I was a baby and with my father gone now, I didn't have any family in town. The small home at the edge of the property where Dad and I lived was torn down after he passed."

"Why? Was it falling down or something?" Hudson asked, his eyes scanning the room as if to see if anything had gone missing.

"No. It was torn down due to a code violation."

He rubbed his forehead. "That house was there before I was born. I don't remember, but I know we lived in that house when I was a baby, before my dad bought the bigger house and moved us north of the city when I was a kid. I'm surprised Nana let that happen."

"She didn't have a choice. The county wanted to put a road in, and apparently the cabin was partially on the property line. Nana fought but then discovered that after your grandfather died and left part of the land to your father in the will, your father sold the property to use the money for his first business deal."

Anger flashed across Hudson's face, but he shook it off, like he'd always shaken off his father's shady tactics. "Does he know that Nana passed? He always said he'd tear this place down and turn the entire town into an investment, wiping out any embarrassing trace of where he'd come from."

"Nana reached out to him when she first got sick, but when he didn't respond she decided she didn't want him knowing about her passing. I respected her wishes and didn't contact anyone but you." Juniper wanted to stay on topic. Now wasn't the time to talk about their childhood together on this farm and how he didn't know anything about it in recent years.

He hadn't lived here for fifteen years. Sure, he'd sneaked to the farm so much after his mother died that his father had given up. Except when his father would get a notion to have Hudson at home for a few weeks here or there, mostly to show him off at some business function or to play the good-father routine to land a deal. But Hudson had been gone since he'd run off after high school, so he had no idea about farm life anymore and how things worked in a small town.

She pushed away the memories to unbox later. For now, she nudged their conversation back on point. "Since my home was gone and Nana was lonely, she insisted I move in here. We grew closer than ever and during our time together we made plans."

Hudson shifted in his seat, obviously losing patience.

Juniper sucked in a deep breath and shot out the important part. "We were going to start a hippotherapy program."

"Hippo what?"

"Hippotherapy. It's an equestrian program for children with disabilities." At the word *children*, she saw him flinch, so she rushed all her words out before he shut her down. "It's a valuable tool in treating children and adults with all different challenges in life. Your Nana pushed me into completing my bachelor's degree in counseling, so I was able to get my equine therapy certification while I took care of her. That allows me to work with people with various mental health needs by caring for horses and leading them around, which is proven to reduce stress and anxiety. But I'll have to hire a physical therapist to do hippotherapy, where people work on physical and emotional challenges while riding a horse.

There are grants for funding and tax breaks that will make this place an asset for a man like you looking for ways to put your money to good use and have a tax write-off. Also, by allowing me to run this program and live here, you'll be able to hold on to your family heritage without ever having to step foot on the farm or needing to return to Willow Oaks again."

"No," he said flatly. "Not interested."

She took a sip of tea and rolled through her mind for other options, but she couldn't think of any. Tears pooled in her eyes, but she wouldn't let him see her cry, so she stood up to find her sweet five-year-old daughter toe-running into the room with open arms.

Hudson's mouth fell open and his eyes went wide. "Who's that?"

Her beautiful little girl ran to him before Juniper could stop her. To her surprise, Gracie, who didn't like strangers, crawled up in his lap and gave him a wet kiss on his cheek, and then cuddled into him. She held her breath, but Hudson didn't squirm or run for the nearest exit. Probably shock.

She hated to have to beg, especially to Hudson, but a mother would do anything for her child. "Please, we have nowhere else to live."

Hudson closed his eyes, then nudged Gracie from his lap and stood, straightening his tie. A flash of childhood trauma and internal struggle showed in his tight-lipped frown. She knew he was conflicted between what his father expected and what his grandmother wanted. “I’m not a monster. There’s the nice apartment over the barn. You can live there while I work on renovating this place. That’ll give you time to find a new home.” He hid his remorseful expression behind his next actionable item, his father’s influence apparently gaining ground. He headed for the study. “Now, where’s the will?”

She had no choice but to accept the only offer on the table and pray she’d come up with another plan since her ex had gambled away most of her money and the attorney fees for the divorce had depleted the rest of her savings. The apartment over the barn wasn’t really an option with all the dangers it presented for Gracie, but Juniper would figure something out.

She scooped Gracie into her arms and followed Hudson into the other room. “The program would help my daughter.” She tried to make him see how important this would be to so many, but he didn’t even bother to respond. Hudson never dealt with feelings. He hid behind work and purpose, the coping mechanisms his father had shamed him into adopting.

In the top drawer of the desk, she pulled out the will and handed it to him.

"Have you read it?"

"No, it wasn't mine to read."

He opened the envelope and unfurled the papers. His face went from sad to perplexed to angry. "What? She says it was her dying wish that I stay here until I restore the farm and that you and I are equal owners of the property but that you'll be residing in the house." His voice boomed, startling Gracie.

Juniper grabbed the will and read over the legal jargon that made little sense, but she caught the main point. Her heart soared to Heaven. "We don't have to leave the farm?"

Hudson snatched it back. "This can't be real. What am I supposed to do?" His gaze bucked from her to the will to the house to Gracie. The internal struggle between his father and grandmother rolled out in front of him and Juniper thought he might collapse with the crack in his cold, carefully constructed foundation.

She offered the sincerest smile, but inside, her joy wasn't so pure. "There's an apartment over the barn you can stay in."

Chapter Two

The wind whipped dust into Hudson's eyes. He swiped away the irritant and yanked open the old barn door. Rust coated his hand from the wrought iron handle and splinters dropped onto his Italian shoes. The smell of old, musty manure and the sight of a hundred cobwebs welcomed him.

The barn stood empty—no horses, barn cats or goats. Faded light beamed through the space between a few decaying slats overhead, making what was once the heart of the farm stand lifeless. Everything felt lifeless without Nana's heartwarming smile and Southern charm filling every inch of the farm.

He eyed the hayloft and the memory of his first kiss tickled his senses. A kiss with June Bug. The flash of his childhood crush sent the hair on the back of his neck into a tango. It was only one kiss, a kiss that his father warned him would ruin his life. The way his father had ruined his own life for many years when he'd married and had a child. A life his father said had held him back far too long, and he didn't want that for Hudson.

The memory faded and he shook off any more thoughts from rearing up by forcing his gaze to the crooked stairs.

His phone shrilled from his pocket, and when he saw the caller ID, he couldn't hit Answer fast enough. "This is your fault."

"What?" Mark Worthington answered. His best friend, together with Hudson, had built their company into the successful business it was today.

"I can't believe you told me to return to Willow Oaks." He eyed the cows through the back window mulling about in the pasture.

"You're doing the right thing. Trust me. You don't want to wait until it's too late to open your heart to the world."

Mark's words made Hudson feel like a crash test dummy hitting the wall of grief hard and fast. "My nana's dead. Passed away a few days ago. I was too late."

"Sorry, man." Mark sounded tired.

"It's what it is." Hudson winced at his own words. He spoke them, but inside, his gut twisted, and his stomach churned. "Are you overdoing it? I should get back there quick."

"I don't think you can overdo dying," Mark

said in the flippant way he'd adopted since receiving his colon cancer diagnosis.

"Funny. Really." Hudson spotted a field mouse running along the beams overhead. "You've got years. Make the best of them. That's what you keep telling me, right?"

"Right. That's why you needed a vacation."

"Vacation?" Hudson trudged up the rickety old stairs, ready to sink into a comfy bed. It had been so long since he'd slept in fresh air with nothing but the crickets and owls to soothe him to sleep. "Nana told me in her will that she wants me to stay here and fix up the farm."

"Great. Maybe you can relax, start a family."

Family? Never. "I like the old, precancer Mark Worthington. The less philosophical workaholic that didn't push his friend to travel hundreds of miles to the nowhere town of his youth. Who uses up their dying request to send their friend to see his grandmother?"

"Because it's the one way you can't refuse." Mark cleared his throat the way he did when he became tired from all the cancer treatments he'd been undergoing.

Hudson longed to do more, but he could only do what he'd promised. "No, I couldn't refuse."

"So, is that girl of yours there? You know, with the funeral I assume she was in town. The one who grew up on the farm with you. The one that

I mentioned you could run into, and your eyes lit up? What was her name? Chrysanthemum?"

"Juniper." His stomach knotted at the thought of the sweet young lady who always brought a light to his dark world. "And she's not my girl. Don't try to bring me to the dark side just because you fell in love."

Hudson reached the landing and found a piece of wood slid across the door resting on two hooks, so he dropped his overnight bag and lifted the plank out of the way to discover a scene from a lost and forgotten childhood.

"About my dying wish… I want you to stay for the next few weeks and work on your family farm. You owe it to your nana." Mark's voice sounded stern but comforting.

"I don't have that kind of time. Besides, Juniper wants to fix up this place to start some hippotherapy program. There's no money in that and I'm not turning Nana's place into some failing business."

"Money isn't everything." Mark coughed, but it sounded forced and cagey. "Stay and help her. It's my final wish."

The line went dead. Apparently, Mark still used his manipulative tricks to get what he wanted. Too bad he didn't direct his tactics back toward the business.

Hudson tossed his phone on a dusty desk. A

chair leaned on its side with one leg busted, and a cracked oval mirror hung crooked on the wall. Everything was covered in grime. What had happened to Nana that she allowed things to get this bad out here? The woman took pride in her hard work and had always kept the farm and home in immaculate condition.

It hit him then: Nana was gone. Gone from the world too soon. Too soon for him to reconcile his guilt of staying away all these years.

The will. What had driven her to play games with his life? Revenge for his absence? No. Nana was strong and determined and loving but never malicious. Something else had caused that decision, but at the moment, he was too tired and too hungry to care. But he knew one thing—he could make amends by restoring this place in honor of Nana. If that was her last wish, he'd make it happen. If nothing else, his entire empire rested on buying and restoring old resorts into magnificent and expensive getaways. For once in his life, he could use his renovation skills from the outside world to honor his childhood here at the farm. His two worlds would finally mesh.

But after he restored the place, then what? He didn't want to sell it, didn't want to turn it into some therapy center with strangers traipsing all over, and he didn't want to live here. Confusion whirled but how could he process any of it when he'd just found out about Nana? It was too much for one afternoon.

He retrieved his bag and set it on the nightstand, then lowered onto the bed. The old-fashioned mattress spit white into the air, and the springs groaned under his weight, warning him the bed could collapse.

Resting his elbows on his knees, he analyzed the ruins of his past life. Tears pricked in the corners of his eyes, but he'd learned a long time ago that men never cried. Not real men. His father had taught him that lesson more than once.

Heat accosted him, causing sweat to drip from his neck to his waist. There was nothing worse than getting hot in a dress shirt and pants, so he cranked the small window open to the sound of giggles.

He peered out and saw little Gracie chasing a butterfly. As if watching an old movie replay in his head, he saw little June Bug skipping and running in the field, chasing flittering creatures and laughing. Gracie, with her bright blue eyes and wild blond hair, was a replica of her mother.

With a deep breath of fresh-cut grass from a neighboring farm, he studied Juniper kneeling at the edge of the garden. Tall stalks of corn and vines of something wrapped around wood poles stuck out of the ground, obstructing his view of her. Only the back of her neck showed, with her hair up on her head revealing her long, thin Audrey Hepburn–esque feature. That was what Nana had called it anyway.

Juniper cut a tomato from a plant with the grace of a bonsai tree pruner. Her delicate fingers held the round object up to the sun and she turned it as if analyzing every shade of red and yellow, reminding him of Nana showing him how to pick the best produce.

An ache welled inside him. He fisted his hand and rubbed his chest, but it didn't relent. His breath caught somewhere between his lungs and his nose, so he unbuttoned his shirt halfway and leaned out to inhale the fresh air. Clean and unspoiled by the pollution of man and machines.

To his disappointment, Juniper called out to Gracie, "Time to get dinner ready."

His stomach growled, but he knew nothing in town would be open, so he returned to the edge of the bed and analyzed the will over and over and over again until his eyes stung, his neck hurt and the smell of hearty spaghetti sauce wafted from the main house.

He knew that smell anywhere. It was his nana's sauce. Oregano and basil filled the air so richly the fragrance coated his tongue, making his mouth water.

A field mouse ran across the weathered boards. Irritation nibbled at him. Why'd Juniper send him out here knowing the condition of the apartment? Sure, he'd suggested she live out here, but he hadn't known it had been left in such a dirty state. This woman wasn't his sweet June Bug. The girl who took the blame when he'd broken his father's hunting trophy to spare him punishment. The girl who'd volunteered to deliver food to the shut-ins in the community. She'd always been the epitome of goodness and righteousness. Another reason he'd pushed her away. No reason to tarnish her soul with his dark spirit.

Who was she now, and how could he get her to agree to sell her half of the farm to him? Maybe the divorce had made her bitter and she was lashing out. Not that he could believe anything Juniper did was less than for the good of others.

Heat seared his skin with regrets. What had happened between his old college roommate and Juniper? Maybe his father was right, and marriage never worked.

His stomach growled louder than a tractor engine turning over, so he decided this was ridiculous. No way he'd stay in this dirty apartment, starving all night.

A long time ago, he would've loved the adventure of staying out here, but he'd softened after years of 1000-count Egyptian cotton and fancy dinners. No dinner ever compared to Nana's spaghetti, though. Certainly, Juniper wouldn't deny him food and a seat at Nana's table. She was as Southern and polite as his nana had been.

He marched across the green grass to the house and hammered his fist against the front door, sending specks of worn yellow paint floating to the ground. Realizing his overkill, he leaned his forehead against the front door.

Gracie screamed and then bellowed her displeasure like a cow in labor. Kids were noisy and strange.

"Just a minute." Juniper's steps hurried closer. When she opened the door, a sour expression on her face, she cuddled a crying Gracie into her leg. "Don't bang like that."

"What?"

She swiped wayward hair strands from her eyes with the back of her hand. "I said… Never mind. What do you want?"

He pointed to the barn. "I thought maybe I could stay in the house tonight. That way, we can speak about our options."

"No." One word, that was all he got from Juniper. The girl who would talk until he couldn't stand it any longer when they were young.

"What?"

"I said no. Nana said that I get to live in the house. Besides, you thought the apartment would be good enough for my daughter and me."

Conviction wiggled into his determination, but

he was used to the finer things in life. "I'm happy to pay for a room in the house."

"I don't want your money. If you want to give me something, give me the farm."

"What about James?" he nudged, wanting to know what happened and if there was any hope of a reconciliation. His heart split in two, part tethered to the past dreams of a happily-ever-after he knew better than to hope for, and the other part tethered to the present where he knew he should get back to work and what mattered in his life. Making money.

Her brows furrowed into a wicked expression. "What about him?"

The door slammed in his face. Gracie cried, and Juniper sang a sweet song until the screams slowed into whimpers. The voice soft and comforting as if welcoming someone home. That was what his nana had said to him once when she'd told him he and Juniper should get married, live together on the farm and raise their own children. An idea as ridiculous today as it was then. He wasn't the marrying kind.

He didn't know who this woman was, but it couldn't be his June Bug. "Fine, I'll stay with a friend."

"You have friends around here?" Juniper's voice carried through the open window.

He struggled between yelling back and letting

it go. But she wasn't wrong. He hadn't spoken to anyone in Willow Oaks in years.

Not wanting to be like his father, causing a child more anguish when she was already upset, he headed to the barn but heard the sound of the front door of the house open, stopping him in his tracks.

He turned, but it slammed shut before he could even catch a glimpse of Juniper. Instead, a container of spaghetti sat on top of some sheets, and Nana's favorite quilt rested on the front porch swing. Next to it a thermos probably of lemonade or tea. "Thank you," he called through the open window.

"Only did it for Nana. She wouldn't want her soft city grandson starving to death."

"Soft? Despite affording the finer things in life that I've worked hard to achieve, I'm not soft. I can still out-chop, out-mow and outlast any farm hand in the area."

When no response came, he grabbed the bedding and dinner and returned to the small, lonely apartment.

In the morning, he'd straighten this out. He'd discover why his grandmother had played this game. Why would she make Juniper half owner of the farm? The only home he ever truly knew growing up. The one place he felt safe and could find happiness away from his father. But when

Juniper had teased the resolve of his vow to remain single, he knew he had to leave.

His life on the farm had been simple and calm. Perhaps this was his chance to recapture the feelings of a life beyond budgets, boardrooms and brutality. His father had a heavy hand, but Hudson, by remaining unmarried and childless, had broken the Kenmore bloodline of overbearing fathers who demanded the impossible from their sons. Broken the unhappy life behind closed doors with the fake smile and lies projected to the outside world.

He savored the hearty spaghetti. The oregano tickling his memories of many happy dinners at Nana's table. Once done, he grabbed the small rug and hung it out the window, smacking it against the side of the barn to free it of all the accumulated dust. As if he beat his heart against the siding, causing his chest to ache and his mind to drift to forgotten possibilities.

Nana would tell him to close his eyes and let the worries fade away because tomorrow would be a brighter day. Only he knew it wouldn't be because his nana wouldn't be there waiting with her hotcakes, sweet smile and warm hugs. After all these years, a part of him longed for that connection. The one he'd felt with his nana and, at one time, he'd felt with Juniper.

Chapter Three

The morning sun shot through the white curtains handmade by Nana. Everything in this house had been created with heart by her, and there was no place in the world Juniper could imagine feeling more like home than this one.

The way the lace splintered the light made it look like Nana watched from Heaven. Juniper's heart ached to feel that connection with someone again. The quiet of the house as Gracie slept unnerved Juniper with the realization of how lonely her life had become. Nana's passing left a huge hole in her, but she had to be strong for Gracie.

Juniper opened the front door to inhale God's gracious gift of clean air and looked to the fields for inspiration, but instead, she eyed the barn. Shame filled her for not inviting him for dinner, but if she let that man into her life again, she'd make the wrong choice over and over again. She refused to think about any man, especially the one who had captured her heart and never let it go.

Southern hospitality was overrated.

She stepped back, ignoring the call to invite him in for breakfast like Nana would've wanted. "Why did you leave this place to both of us?"

A soft snore sounded from Gracie's room, reminding Juniper that she didn't have long before her little flying squirrel took flight, so she settled in for her morning devotion with Nana's Bible. A tradition they had started together when Nana took to her bed in the final months of her life.

Juniper closed her eyes, opened the Bible, flipped the pages and stuck her finger on a passage. She peered out through her lashes to find knowledge to follow today when she felt so lost and alone. As if Nana were by her side, she read aloud, "Ezekiel 36:26. 'A new heart also will I give you, and a new spirit will I put within you: and I will take away the stony heart out of your flesh, and I will give you a heart of flesh.'"

Wind whistled through the front screen, warning a storm might be coming. Conviction took hold, but she shut the book, looked to the ceiling and said, "Okay, but all I can do is the work to soften my heart to welcome him into your home the way you would want. I'll do it for you and because God says to open my heart, but I don't like it." She set the Bible on the side table next to the rocker and headed to the kitchen.

She opened a whitewashed Shaker cabinet, pulled out Nana's cast-iron skillet and studied the bits of seasoning as if to find answers. "Couldn't you have sent something easier?"

"Sent what?" Hudson's deep voice jolted her. The heavy pan slipped from her hands.

Ca-clang!

"Maaaammmmaaa!" Gracie screeched from her room.

Juniper grabbed her chest as if to keep her heart from leaping out of her body from the startle. "What're you doing in here? How did you get inside?" she squealed in irritation.

"The front door was open, and the screen door was unlocked."

She shot by a disheveled Hudson with his hands raised in surrender. "Coming, Gracie. It's okay."

She rushed to her daughter's room to find her under the desk with her palms pressed to her ears. "It's okay, darlin'. I dropped a pan."

Gracie rocked several more times and hummed. Poor girl, she'd come such a long way before the therapy stopped, because the money stopped, because her life stopped. All because of a gambling addiction and poor choices. *Dear Lord, why is life a continuous test?*

"What's wrong with her?" Hudson asked.

His judgmental words irked Juniper, but she kept her eyes on Gracie and outstretched her arms, welcoming her for a cuddle. "Nothing's wrong with her. She has some sensory challenges, that's all."

She dared a glance at Hudson, who leaned against the doorjamb, running his hand through his hair, dark scruff dotting his chin and cheeks. The man looked comfortable in any situation, even when he shouldn't. *Nana, is this seriously what you want?*

Gracie crawled out and tucked herself into a ball in Juniper's arms. "Mama's got you," Juniper murmured, rocking her little squirrel. She caressed her daughter's silky hair and held her tight until she calmed, and her tense little frame relaxed.

Gracie popped up like a clown out of a jack-in-the-box and stood on her toes. "Cakes?" Her eyes shone with such hope, and her little frame was straight like she stood at attention with ballerina feet.

"Sure."

Gracie ran on her tippy toes to Hudson, her little fists pulled to her shoulders and shaking in glee. "Pa-cakes!"

He lowered to a squat. "I heard. Is that your favorite?"

"Uh-huh, uh-huh."

"Mine, too." Hudson met Juniper's gaze. "Boy, I'd love some pancakes."

"Stay." Gracie took his hand in hers and tugged on him to follow her.

Juniper looked to the ceiling. "Pulling out the big guns now, huh?" She let out a long sigh and realized she'd gotten exactly what she'd missed most, someone to fill the emptiness from the loss of Nana. Sure, maybe she was Hudson's biological grandmother, but Nana had said long ago there was enough of her love to go around. The woman had been there when Juniper's own family had gone from this earth or from her life.

She pushed from the floor and smacked into Hudson's chest. A sharp breath and jolt of heat flashed across her skin.

"Who were you talking to?"

Juniper swallowed back her words, knowing Hudson would think she'd lost her ever-lovin' mind if she told him she was talking to Nana. "God."

Hudson scoffed. "You still believe in God after all you've been through?"

"Of course. You don't?"

He shrugged. "I work hard and earn what I want in life. I don't rely on asking for things from anyone, not even God."

Juniper winced at his words. "That's your father talking."

"He's the reason I'm so successful today." The way Hudson lifted his chin was more in defiance than pride. He'd always wanted to prove his father wrong about him being worthless and his grandmother wrong for saying he was softhearted, despite the fact that she'd meant it as a compliment.

Juniper brushed past him, wanting to gain some space and perspective since Hudson always had a way of turning her around. "I guess you were right all those years ago."

"About what?" He followed on her heels past Gracie sitting crisscross applesauce in front of the television with Little Einsteins playing their happy tune.

"That you weren't the marrying kind. That you'd never be anything more than what your father had been to you, so you would never have children or a wife or a future."

His footsteps stopped padding after her, but she kept walking into the kitchen, leaving him behind, the way he'd left her behind all those years ago.

He came in and took a seat at the kitchen table, eyeing her as she retrieved eggs, milk and flour. "When did you become so bitter and harsh?"

"Bitterness would imply that I care, and I don't. I was simply stating facts. That's what you business types know the best, right? Numbers and facts." She decided she wouldn't be his servant, and he could work for anything he wanted the old-fashioned way. The way his nana had raised them. She opened the side drawer and tossed an apron at him. "You want to eat, you can cook."

Hudson took the apron and slid the ruffled neck over his head. What a sight, the almighty and wealthy man in his nana's apron, cooking pancakes. Now, that was a man Juniper could care about. Not that she intended on caring about another man ever again.

"Was it money? If so, I can offer James a good job," Hudson said as if discussing the apple tree growing outside the kitchen window.

She whipped the pancake batter into submission until Hudson covered her hand with his, catching her attention and her breath. She surrendered the bowl to him. "It wouldn't do any good."

Gracie giggled. The sound meant Juniper and Hudson were free to talk. As long as the singing and dancing characters continued, Gracie was happy and mesmerized for a few minutes. "You think I spent his money or that I was a lazy wife or something?"

Hudson cleared his throat and poured batter into the bubbling oil. "Ah, no. I mean—"

"I knew that would be your first thought. You never did think highly of me." Juniper spun on her heels, but he caught her arm and turned her back to face him.

His eyes were wide and full of something she couldn't define. Sorrow? Regrets? She wasn't sure.

"I've never thought that about you, ever. If anything, I always thought you were too good for me," he said.

She eyed his grasp on her bicep, and he let go, returning to his pancakes.

"Could he not handle Gracie's, er, um…challenges?"

Juniper's temper sparked. "No, he couldn't, but it's worse than that. For your information, he gambled away all our money and now I can't even afford therapy for Gracie."

Hudson visibly winced. His mouth drew into his thin, angry frown. After a few seconds, he returned to watching the pancake batter bubble in the pan. "That's why you wanted to start the program." Hudson nodded as if he understood everything in her world after five minutes.

He flipped the pancakes and then set the spatula down. "Tell you what. I'll buy the place from you. Then you'll have all the money you need."

Juniper eyed the dangling promise of financial security. "Then what?"

"What do you mean?"

"What will you do with this place once you buy it from me?"

Hudson shrugged. "Don't know."

Everything inside Juniper told her to take the money and run so she could provide a better future for Gracie, but she couldn't. Nana would be heartbroken if Hudson sold the farm. "No. I won't accept your guilt money. Not because I don't need it, but Nana wanted me and Gracie to have this as our home. I know she was your grandmother, but I became her only family for many years."

He stiffened as if she'd shocked him into actually listening for a change. She stepped into his personal space to make him hear the real truth. For once, she had something to say to him. "This place is the only thing that should matter to you, but instead, for most of your adult life you chose fancy, stale resorts over your family home. You'll have to find another way to run me out of your life again. It shouldn't be too hard—you're good at pushing people away."

"I never meant to hurt you, June Bug." He brushed a strand of hair behind her ear and looked down with those large blue eyes with *I'm sorry* etched in his gaze.

"I'm not your June Bug, and I'm not talking about me. You pushed everyone out of your life, including Nana."

"I didn't—"

"You did. It took your nana calling to ask you for help to get you here."

"How do you know about that?"

"Who do you think convinced her to make the call? It was her last wish to see her grandson before she died. If only you would've come home immediately… But I'm sure another big deal of yours couldn't wait. Money has meant, and always will mean, more to you than family."

Hudson's gut tied into a constrictor knot. Juniper's words were like dry ice on his soul. "You're right." He turned to the pancakes Nana had taught him to make, unable to face the judgment in Juniper's eyes. Shame coated him like molasses, sticky goo he'd never be able to shake off.

His mind raced as if he stood in his boardroom knowing his next words either closed a big deal or lost it forever. Forever was a long time. He needed to make this right, both for Juniper and to honor his grandmother.

Juniper simmered behind him, and he knew he needed a plan before he faced her again. She was the one person who always stirred him up inside and made him doubt his choices. He'd doubted himself the most when he'd introduced her to James. Obviously, that wasn't his best decision.

He needed to convince her that it would be best for Gracie if she took the money and moved on to a more suitable place for them. He closed his eyes and readied himself to present an offer she couldn't refuse. Everyone had a price. But when he spun around to face her, she'd disappeared from the room. A room that once felt full of life, now vacant and quiet.

Giggles sounded from the living room along with claps. That little girl could fill a universe with her charm. He shook off the thought, finished plating all the pancakes and set them on the table. "Breakfast is ready."

Gracie shot into the room on her toes and hugged his leg but didn't say anything. He deciphered that was her way of saying thank-you. He brushed her soft, thin, blond hair away from her face. "You're welcome."

She bounced to the table and crawled up onto the old wooden and wicker chair to tear apart and shove a quarter of a pancake in her mouth.

Juniper walked in and calmly sat by her side and held up a fork. "Remember, we need to use our utensils when we eat."

Gracie shook her head. "Nuh-huh. Nuh-huh."

A flash of a memory from his childhood with Nana feeding a child. It wasn't him, it was a toddler, probably someone she'd watched for a neighbor, but he took hold of the memory and sat down on the other side of Gracie. "Oh no, here comes a train. It needs a place to pull into the station." He took her tiny hand in his, pierced a piece of pancake and lifted it up in the air. "Chaga-chaga. Chaga-chaga, choo-choo!" She giggled and opened her mouth wide to accept the proffered food.

Juniper sat back in her chair and crossed her arms over her chest. "Well, I never."

"Never what?" he asked, stabbing another piece and repeating the Nana move.

"Never thought I'd hear Stone-Cold Hudson choo-chooing."

Those words pinched his pride. "I'm not always cold. Sometimes I do things because I know it's the right thing. It doesn't mean I'm heartless. It means I'm trying to protect those around me."

"More. More." Gracie bounced up and down in her seat.

"You do one, then I'll do one."

"No, more." She tossed her fork, sending syrup drops across the table.

Hudson didn't know what to do with a temper tantrum except fire the employee. He couldn't fire Gracie.

"No, ma'am. We don't toss things, remember?" Juniper picked up the fork. "I know it's hard to hold, but you can do it."

Gracie bowed her head and crossed her arms over her chest. The girl was stubborn like Hudson. He could appreciate that. A compromise so she felt like she still had a voice might work. "Tell you what. You do it once and I'll do it twice. Sound good?"

"Uh-huh, uh-huh." She shot up and grabbed the fork from Juniper in a fist and stabbed three times until she managed to get the pancake onto the fork. Her mouth formed a big O and her hand gripped so tight it shook, sending the piece to splat against her plate an inch from her mouth. She tossed the fork down and cried big tears.

He froze. He was out of ideas.

"She needs something with a bigger handle," Juniper offered with a you-don't-have-a-clue frown. She pulled out a basket from the shelf and handed him a foam tube. "Slide that onto her fork."

"No. For babies." Gracie crossed her arms and puffed out her lip.

Memories flooded in of him running to his nana's house when his father had a particularly bad day. She'd always cheer him up with what she called a Lesson and Blessing. She'd make special cookies and they'd build forts in the living room where he could go away on a Lesson and Blessing adventure. Adventures with Nana and Juniper. His skin warmed. He held up one finger. "No, it's a special blessing," he said in a tone filled with wonder, and he waved his hand toward the ceiling like Nana used to.

Gracie bounced on her knees and clapped. "Bless. Bless."

Juniper raised a brow. "Try it once together."

Gracie clapped with her palms, fingers bent outward. He sat by her side and covered her hand with his. "Bless this special gift and take us on an adventure." They stabbed a piece of pancake and she gasped with delight.

His heart warmed with accomplishment and from her glee.

"Choo-choo." Her little light eyebrows shot up so high with the question, he didn't have to doubt what she wanted.

"Chaga-chaga. Chaga-chaga. Choo-choo."

She took the pancake and chewed it up, then stabbed at another piece. Her fork paused and she eyed Hudson.

"Right. Chaga-chaga. Chaga-chaga. Choo-choo."

Gracie made the train reach the station and then dropped her fork and covered her mouth as if scared the food would fall out, squeals escaping through her fingers. Her wide eyes looked to the fork, looked to him, looked to her mother who had tears in her eyes.

The sight made the hair on his arms stand up more than when he'd closed the largest resort deal in the Caribbean, making his partner and him millions.

Juniper cleared her throat and hugged Gracie before sliding away to wash the batter bowl.

He reached for the fork, but Gracie shook her head. "I do. I do."

"Yes, you do." Hudson patted her on the head.

He wasn't sure what just happened, but it appeared to be a big moment.

Hudson went to the sink and found Juniper with tears streaking her cheeks. He rubbed small circles on her back, wanting to soothe whatever he'd done to cause her pain. "I'm sorry."

"No. It's good. You have no idea what you just did," she whispered. "And you used… Lessons and Blessings to do it."

"What did I do?"

She sniffled and sponged off the bowl like she was scrubbing rust from an old pipe. "You were able to get Gracie to do what she hasn't done since Nana got too sick to eat with her at the table. I never thought Hudson Kenmore would offer his time to a little girl, especially when her own father wouldn't even help."

Her wavering voice choked his resolve to stay driven and focused on what was important. He'd forgotten how Juniper could soften him to the point of wanting to give up his life to stay with her. But that would end badly. The way his father and mother had ended badly.

"I'm sorry. When I introduced you to James, I did so because I thought he'd make you happy."

She chuckled, not a sound of joy but of challenge.

"What?"

She turned off the water and eyed Gracie still working on her pancakes.

"Is that what you tell yourself?"

Gracie stopped and eyed them, so he made the choo-choo noise, and she continued. "What are you talking about?"

She tossed a towel at him and handed him the bowl. "You introduced us to shove me from your life permanently. You'd closed yourself off from love for so long, and you were too scared to take a chance on anything but the safety of working the next deal."

"I—I—"

"Dig deep, Hudson. You'll know it's true."

Conviction sent a chill down his spine. "I'm sorry James turned into a gambling fool."

"No. Me marrying James you can't take credit for. That's my mistake. I wanted to move on with my life when I realized we'd never be together. That poor choice was mine. However, I don't regret it."

"Why's that? Look at what's happened to you."

"Yes, look what happened to me. I have a beautiful and amazing daughter. God blessed me with more than I ever thought I'd have in my life."

He dried the bowl but remained at her side as if waiting in line to purchase something. "I don't see how you can still be into God when this is all He has to offer. I've done better without Him."

"Have you?" Juniper put her palm to his chest, and it was like he could feel her touching his heart. "How happy are you? You still live your life with fear of commitment. You can't even commit to fixing up this place with me despite Nana's wishes."

She withdrew her comfort and left him to face her words. Words that spoke the truth despite how hard he tried to deny it. Had he become more like his father, driving people away while trying to protect them, only to fail them with his absence? He didn't even make it home to say goodbye to the one adult in his life who'd treated him with kindness. Made him feel loved. He'd failed her over and over again. Did she even know how much she'd meant to him?

Juniper was right, he owed it to his grandmother. It was too late to tell Nana how he felt, but he could honor her wishes in a vain attempt to make it up to her, no matter how strange her request. He owed it to her for all she'd done for him in his youth. "Let's do it."

"Do what?"

Hudson rocked back on his heels and put his hands on his hips, already making a mental note of the repairs needed in the kitchen. Mark had made his wish, and he had no choice but to grant it. He'd already failed Nana before she passed, he couldn't fail his best friend, too. "Fix up the farm together. I want to honor Nana's wishes and restore this place. After we're done, the property will be worth more. Then you can sell your half to me."

"Not going to happen. I'm going to run my horse therapy programs here when we're done."

He shrugged. "Or you'll realize that you and Gracie would be better off taking the money."

She opened her mouth, but he held up his palm. "We'll table that discussion for the moment." But the way she swished her lips and popped her hip warned she was about to start an epic battle right now.

His phone buzzed in his pocket, so he used the distraction to give her a minute to think before their conversation took a right turn to the wrong destination. But when he pulled his phone out, he saw his father's personal number pop up. He sucked in a quick breath. "It's my father."

That snapped Juniper out of all anger and into a wide-eyed look of fear. "Answer it."

He cleared his throat and answered. "Hello?"

"Time for you to stop your madness and work for me. I'm offering junior partnership of Kenmore Enterprises. We'll combine our companies and be the largest in the world." His voice boomed with his orders, but Hudson wouldn't bend. Not now, not ever.

"No."

The phone went dead but it set Hudson's nerves into a frenzy.

"What is it?" Juniper stepped closer.

Hudson shrugged. "Another command for me to go to work for my father."

His phone buzzed with a text.

Meeting pushed. Had to go. Call me back in a few hours.

"You sure no one told him about Nana's passing?" His stomach churned with worry.

"I didn't," Juniper said but her gaze went to the window. "But I can't guarantee no one in town did."

Hudson tried to call his father back to see what he knew, but he didn't answer. Not that night nor the next morning, which only made him more nervous because he couldn't help but think his father would show up and order them all off the land and tear away everything that had ever made him or Juniper happy.

Chapter Four

Juniper scooped Gracie out of her car seat and lowered her to the sidewalk in front of Bless Your Heart Café. After three long tension-filled days of Hudson wiggling his way into meals and having to use the house bathroom and other intrusions into their life, she welcomed the escape into town. Not to mention the waiting game to hear from his father. Dear Lord, what did he want? Would he contest the will and would she and Gracie be out of a home? The man had a legion of lawyers.

She shook her head to push away thoughts of Hudson. She needed a breath, a chance to forget about the man she'd once adored and wanted in her life. "Ma. I-ceam?"

Juniper shook off the thought. "Ice cream is reserved for a special treat for special little girls." She retrieved the basket of fresh produce, eggs and flowers, shut the door and took Gracie's hand.

"I good." She marched with high knees up to

the florist shop but let go of Juniper's hand the minute the bell jingled overhead. "Mi-mi."

"Hi, sweet girl." Mindi threw Gracie up in the air and caught her, causing squeals and giggles.

It warmed Juniper's heart to see Gracie smile. She loved Mindi, but coming into town could be a huge stress on her and Gracie with all the unknown variables. Here, in the florist shop, it would be safe, though. "Brought some flowers for you."

Mindi might be five years younger, but she'd always been more mature than even the elders of this town. She had to be, to care for her younger siblings after her father went to jail.

"Thanks. So, Hudson crashing with you at the farm?" she asked in a *k-i-s-s-i-n-g* tone.

"Grow up." Juniper set the bundle of wildflowers down on the front desk, fulfilling her weekly order to the shop. The chore only provided a few extra dollars, but every bit helped.

Mindi shrugged and flipped her blue hair behind her shoulder. "How you doing?"

"Fine."

Mindi tilted her head, her eyebrow ring glinting in the early morning light. "Spill. I'm the only vault in this town."

Juniper sighed and shooed a running Gracie into the corner and handed her a vase and some flowers so she could mimic Mindi, who placed the wildflowers around some roses in a display. "Nana left the farm to us both, Hudson and me."

Mindi chuckled. "Sounds like good ol' Nana. She always wanted her grandson and you to be together."

"Not going to happen." Juniper grabbed the basket of vegetables and held out her hand to Gracie, but she knew it would be pointless to rush the little girl out. Gracie couldn't abandon something before it was complete. To avoid a tantrum, Juniper accepted her fate and joined them in making bouquets.

"You know Hudson's not James, right?" Mindi asked.

"Not even in the same town." Juniper rolled her eyes. "I know what you're doing, though. You think I'll close myself off from Hudson because I've been hurt by James."

"No, I think you'll close yourself off because Hudson was the one who hurt you. James has been a speed bump on your life road."

Juniper shook her head and willed Gracie to work faster. "You and your feel-good stuff. Speaking of feeling good, are you doing the singles retreat this weekend?"

"Nice deflection. Yes, I'm running the event." Mindi smiled an I've-got-news smile.

"What?"

She shrugged. "It's nothing. Just that Pastor

John asked me to go to dinner tonight to speak about the event."

"Whoa, finally."

"Stop." She abandoned her arrangement and faced Juniper. "I'm not going."

"Why?"

"Because. Have you seen me? I'm not exactly pastor girlfriend material. The elders will need oxygen if they see us together."

"God doesn't care that you have blue hair, and you're happy in your skin, so go for it. You don't need to change for anyone because you're awesome the way you are."

Mindi smiled, and Juniper saw the trap snapping shut. "I'll go for it with Pastor John when you open your heart to the possibilities with Hudson Kenmore."

Despite Gracie still having three flowers left to arrange, Juniper nudged her away, causing her to erupt in a mega fit.

Gracie didn't calm until they reached the edge of the farm, forgoing the short car nap she usually got during Juniper's errands. That wouldn't be good later.

Juniper cut off the engine and said a silent prayer to be a better mother. She'd lost her cool and had to remember Gracie needed things just the right way if she was to continue improving, so she unbuckled the car seat and offered her daughter a sweet smile. "Are we going to be a good girl and help me fix the fence around the corral so that we can have a place for our horse program?"

Gracie nodded twice. "Uh-huh. Uh-huh." She grabbed Juniper's cheeks and planted a wet, sloppy kiss on her face. "I sorry."

"I'm sorry, too. I should've let you finish your arrangement. If you forgive me for not following the rules, I'll forgive you for a tantrum. Deal?"

"Uh-huh. Uh-huh. Deal." She smiled and kicked her feet in excitement.

Juniper set her on the ground by the truck and she took off for the front porch. "Let's get changed and then we'll get to work."

After she helped Gracie into her favorite galoshes, Juniper grabbed her supplies and headed out to get to work. She held tight to her toolbox with one hand and the loop on Gracie's backpack with the other. Gracie slid her hammer out of her tiny pink Barbie tool belt and waved it in the air with enthusiasm. Juniper wished she could feel her daughter's joy at facing the broken timbers and the rusted metal gate hinges enclosing the horse arena.

They'd need this as well as the barn as a start to make the dream of hippotherapy a reality.

If Nana was here, she'd tell Juniper to concentrate on what she could control and let God take care of the rest, so that was what she did. "Come on, we've got work to do."

Juniper opened the gate and let go of Gracie, relieved to allow her to run free without worrying about her disappearing. She'd stay inside the fenced area, or at least she'd pause before escaping between the wood beams long enough for Juniper to catch her. "You start there, and make sure to hammer the wood good."

"Uh-huh. Uh-huh." Gracie unhooked her tool belt and dropped it on the ground, then squatted in her pink galoshes and hammered away.

Juniper kept one eye on her, though, not wanting to take a chance. If only this place had a ten-foot wall surrounding it. Not that it would stop Gracie from escaping; she'd still find a way out. Her little flying squirrel could climb, jump, shimmy in, under and around anything.

Juniper shook off her fear and went to work on the major issue first—the fence gate. With the toolbox abandoned to the side for now, she squatted to use her leg muscles and heave the wood up an inch to see if she could lift it. To her delight, she could, but it would be a long day and she'd be exhausted around the time Gracie would get her second wind.

A hummingbird fluttered over to the wildflowers at a post near Gracie, and she squealed with delight. "Remember, stay inside the fence," Juniper called to her.

Gracie nodded three times.

The aroma of fresh-cut fields rolled in from nearby, reminding her how many people encroached on this land and wanted to buy her out. She wouldn't sell, though. She'd fight each and every one of them, including Hudson, to keep this farm.

With more determination than ever, she heaved the wood up, balancing it on her shoulder. Bent over and crouched, she managed to hold the nail up to the post, slide her hand to her belt, grab the hammer and drive it home.

Whack.

Pain shot from her thumb. She hollered and dropped the board, falling back into the sand on her backside, tears welling up in her eyes.

"Mama! Mama! Mama!" Gracie was at her side, both her palms pressed to Juniper's face, kissing her cheeks and head and nose. "Okay? Okay? Okay?"

The sting still took her words, but she managed to let her thumb go and wrap her arms around Gracie. "I'm always good when you give me hugs and kisses."

Gracie tightened her little arms around Juniper's neck, squeezing her tight. "Now I'm all better from my special Gracie medicine."

"Uh-huh, uh-huh." Gracie kissed her several more times.

"Need some help with that?" Hudson's voice broke through her moment with Gracie, who spotted a butterfly and took off.

"Remember, stay in the fenced area," Juniper hollered after her.

Juniper's pulse skipped and skidded to a stop at Hudson's Italian leather shoes, dress pants and button-up shirt, his attire more suited for a ball than farm work.

"So, do you want help?"

"I'm good," Juniper choked out, ignoring the draw to him she'd been able to deny from a distance up until now.

She thought about having him roll up his sleeves just to see him sweat, but decided she wouldn't accept his help because it would only give him leverage to prove she couldn't run the horse programs and this farm on her own.

"You don't look like you're good."

"Gee, thanks."

He climbed over the lower slat and offered his hand. "Stop being so stubborn."

She took his hand and stood, brushing the dirt from her backside. "Me, stubborn? You're the star rider of that bull."

"Maybe so, but listen—you can't possibly do all this work alone."

"I'm not going to sell my half to you when we're done, so you should give up and go home, Hudson. I don't know why you want the property anyway. It's not like living here is conducive to your getting rich mantra."

He looked at the house, then the barn. "No, but it's my nana's place and I was thinking this would be an ideal location to rest in between big deals. A place to decompress."

She shook her head. "You want a vacation home, but I want this place to *be* my home. I've got all I want here. My home, my barn, my daughter." She turned to point to Gracie, but she wasn't there. A sliver of blond hair glistened in the sun near the woods. The woods that led to the pond. "Gracie!"

Terror shot through her like a lightning bolt through a chain-link fence, jolting her into a full run. Hudson reached her by the other end of the arena. "Calm down. We'll catch her."

Juniper didn't stop but shouted at him, "She can't swim."

Hudson bolted past her, vaulted the fence and raced down the path. Juniper slid between the slats, her heart and pulse and fear pounding against every nerve in her body. "Gracie! Stop!"

She didn't care if she startled her daughter as long as she saved her from the danger of the water. The thick brush would be faster than the trail, so she blazed through, shoving the thorny bushes out of the way, tripping over roots and rocks until she stumbled free at the edge of the pond, where she found Gracie tucked into Hudson's arms.

A sight more beautiful than the sunrise over the mountains on a crisp winter morning. She reached out with trembling hands, but Hudson turned Gracie from her and shook his head. "Take a breath and get cleaned up. I've got her."

Juniper clawed at his sleeve to pull Gracie into her arms but noticed blood oozing from her hands and arms.

She swallowed down the cry threatening to scare Gracie and took a step back.

Hudson bounced a sniffling Gracie. "Hey, I'm thinking it's pancake time." He gave a head tilt toward the path and Juniper headed that way, ignoring every ounce of her motherly instinct to pull Gracie into her and never let her go. But she didn't want to upset her, so she walked home, allowing Hudson to carry her.

His deep, soft tone echoed through the woods, soothing her anxiety and fear. Besides Nana, Juniper had been the only one to ever care for Gracie. When Nana passed, Juniper was left to be mother, father, grandmother, caregiver, protector and all other jobs alone. For the briefest of moments, she allowed herself to believe someone else had her little girl while she took a break and a breath.

They reached the house, and she rushed into the bathroom to discover blood trickling from her temple, leaves sticking out from her hair and her shirt torn at the neck. Hudson was right to keep Gracie from seeing her.

Little Einsteins blared from the other room and Hudson's heavy steps sounded from the hallway.

"She's going to watch television for a few minutes while I make some pancakes." He appeared in the mirror behind her, his gaze studying the cuts on her face. "Come, let's get you cleaned up."

He guided her to sit on the chair Nana used in the bathroom when she'd grown too weak to stand. The faucet squealed when it cut on and then Hudson knelt in front of her, dabbing at the stinging cuts one at a time. His gentle touch was as soft as a butterfly wing against her skin.

"Take a breath. Everything's fine." He took one of her hands and held it tight, his gaze locked on hers.

Humbled and confused, she didn't know what to say except, "Thank you." Her voice cracked as did her facade to remain the toughest girl in Georgia.

"Can I ask what exactly Gracie's challenges are?"

Juniper closed her eyes for a moment. How

much should she tell him? All of it, so he'd know why he should run while he could. Like James had. "When she was two, she was diagnosed with autism spectrum disorder."

He held her hand, wiping away smears of blood. "I don't know what that means except that there's a developmental problem."

The light overhead flickered, warning Juniper she needed to change the bulb before it caused Gracie to have an episode. "She's sensitive to many things like lights and sounds."

Hudson glanced at the flicker and nodded as if he understood.

"But she seeks physical touch and movement."

He finished wiping off the last of the blood on her right hand and rinsed the rag. "I'm sorry to ask this, but I knew a child who was autistic and didn't like to be touched. So, this is different?"

If Juniper didn't know better, she'd think Hudson really cared. Maybe Nana had rubbed off on him more than his father had. "Yes, it's different. She likes tight hugs more than anything. Well, except sweets."

He returned to kneeling in front of Juniper and wiped the scrapes on her other hand. "That's not a bad thing."

"She's also not good with transitioning between activities or with life changes. She regressed when we moved here a few years ago after the divorce. She recovered but her speech regressed again once Nana became too weak to get out of bed." Juniper glanced up and found Hudson looking at her with soft eyes and a small encouraging smile, so she dared to continue. "She's also considered a flight risk. That's why there's extra locks on the doors. At some point, I'd like to install an alarm system so I can take a shower without one eye remaining outside the shower curtain at all times."

Gracie at the side of the pond flashed. Tears slid down her cheeks and Hudson dabbed them away. "I know better than to take my eyes off her."

"I didn't do anything. Gracie was a good girl and had stopped at the water's edge before I got there. She said sorry and opened her arms. I swept her up and you were there a second later. Farms can be dangerous for any children let alone a child who tends to run off."

Juniper stiffened and realized how stupid she'd been. She yanked the rag from him, then shot up and faced herself in the mirror. "I'm all she's got, and it's my job to keep her safe. I know what you're going to say. You're gonna tell me this is why I can't start the hippotherapy program, because I need to sell and take the money to put Gracie in some facility where she'll be safe. I've heard it all before—"

"Never. Gracie belongs with you. Not some facility." His words surprised her. The man who didn't want any entanglements and believed in business over all didn't think Gracie should be sent away.

"I'm sorry. I didn't mean to—"

"I'm the one who's sorry." Hudson turned her to face him. "You wouldn't be in this mess if I hadn't pushed James on you."

Juniper chuckled. Not from laughter but from exasperation. "You, Hudson Kenmore, might think you can control people, but you can't. I chose James, not you. Get over yourself. You've done plenty wrong, but my marriage to James isn't one of them."

Her head spun, her stomach rolled and she didn't know which way to turn. But she knew which way not to turn, so she swallowed down the desire to fall into Hudson's arms and believe he could save the day, because her childhood dreams were never going to be a reality and she had Gracie to think of. "I'm fine. And as for Gracie, I'll make sure next time to keep my eyes on her."

"I'm here. We're going to work together. I can help with Gracie while we work on the reno."

"No." Juniper forced a calm to her exterior and lifted her chin, slipping a step away from Hudson's promise of protection, but her insides were still trembling. "Gracie's my responsibility, and the last thing she needs is another disappearing father figure. Go make those pancakes you promised. I'll be out in a couple of minutes."

Hudson ran a hand through his hair and stepped backward into the hallway. "Fine. If that's how you want it."

"It's how I want it." She closed the door and collapsed into the chair, face in hands, and took several deep breaths to fight the welling emotions threatening to surface.

She'd held it together when James had lost their money, she'd held it together when Nana passed away and she held it together when she faced homelessness. So why did she crumble with one gentle touch from Hudson Kenmore?

Hudson spent all day making a list of things they'd need for the barn and exterior of the house, inspecting drains and roof shingles. Before he went to sleep, he tried his father again but no answer. Maybe it was a coincidence that he called. The only problem with that was Hudson didn't believe in coincidences. So, the next morning, when his father didn't answer his cell for the gazillionth time, Hudson resorted to calling his father's secretary.

"Hello, Kenmore Enterprises."

"Hello, is Arthur Kenmore there? This is his son, Hudson."

"Hi, Hudson. Listen, your father told me you might be looking for him, but he said he'd call you when he returned. He's off on a big, important business deal overseas and can't talk now."

Overseas? His anxiety lowered a notch on the familial anxiety ladder. "Do you know what he wants?"

"Sorry, I couldn't say."

The phone clicked and Hudson took in a long breath. If his father was too busy to even return a call, hopefully he was too busy to discover Nana's passing. He'd been paranoid, that's all, so he decided to focus on the interior of the house.

Juniper took Gracie outside the minute breakfast dishes were done. Something told Hudson she didn't want to be in the house with him for too long.

He settled in at Nana's desk and eyed the will one last time. There had to be a loophole. He should be able to buy Juniper out for her own good, but something held him back from taking it to a lawyer. Respect for his nana's wishes. His father would be disappointed in him, but this was Nana's place, and it was the only home in the world his father never ruled over.

Gracie's giggles wafted in on the wind along with the fresh smell of roses from the garden out front. Juniper had always kept a flower garden since she'd learned how to plant when she was seven.

He folded the will and opened the drawer to return it before Juniper might see him and think he was trying to push her out behind her back, only causing her to anger more. Not that he knew why he had made her mad earlier. She'd always been a complex puzzle he couldn't solve.

Inside the drawer, he spotted a letter with *Hudson* written on the outside in his grandmother's writing. He sucked in a quick breath. Had she spelled out her dying wishes further to him? Sorrow welled up inside him, and he hated himself because Juniper was right—he'd finished his big deal before coming home, which had cost him saying goodbye to the one person in the world who'd offered him love in his life when he was growing up.

Not that restoring this place made up for that, but it gave him one thing to honor the woman who'd been his everything during his childhood.

He slid the letter out but held it in his hands for a moment, unsure he wanted to read the message inside. He'd failed her. The woman who'd always been there for him. And now he had to face the fact that he wasn't his own man. He had indeed become his heartless father.

With a loud, deep breath in and then out, he unfolded the paper and read his Nana's final words to him.

My Dearest Grandson,
I want you to know that I'm so proud of the man you are. An honest, hardworking, giving man who would never turn his back on someone who needs help. I'm sorry that I sent for you too late, but I didn't want you to come home and see me wither away, because I knew it would be too difficult after you watched your mother fade from this world, after so many losses in your life, more than you even remember. However, you've always been in my thoughts and prayers, and I've missed you every day.

Over the years, I've watched you struggle between the man you want to be to prove your father wrong, and the man I know you to be that you've denied. You've never truly believed yourself worthy and that's what has kept you from the love of your life.

In your fear of being a bad father, you've crippled your ability to find true happiness. You broke a young woman's heart when you encouraged her to marry her now ex-husband because you would never love her. A lie you told her and yourself because I know you have loved Juniper your entire life. But your desire to be a protector—the way you protected your mother—and to be a good man warred with each other. The two halves you've split into need to mend, and you need to open your heart. Because, dearest grandson, you are the one that has suffered the most from your actions. Yes, you hurt Juniper, but more than that, you've hurt yourself.

Take these next months to restore not only your home but your heart.

I love you more than anything, so I'll be watching from Heaven, waiting for you to finally be the man I know you to be.

Love,
Nana

His hands fell to his lap as if her words were too heavy to hold up any longer. Nana was right. He'd been callous with Juniper's feelings. He needed to do what was right and make up for his misguidance and heartless rejection. But that was all. He wasn't the man to marry, and he certainly wouldn't be a good father. He'd already made Gracie cry with his door pounding. A direct play out of his father's bullying book.

But what did she mean by more loss than he even remembered?

He glanced down at the letter to find more information, but all he saw left was a Bible verse scribbled at the bottom of the page.

Matthew 19:14—But Jesus said, Suffer little children, and forbid them not to come unto me: for of such is the kingdom of heaven.

"Nana, I have no clue what you mean, but I'm going to make things right. I promise."

The front door squealed open, so he shoved the letter into the drawer and swiped his face clear of any emotion.

Gracie came skipping inside, crawled up into his lap and held out purple wildflowers. "You," she said with a heartwarming smile.

And she did warm his heart, melting the glacier with her little arms wrapping around his neck. For the briefest of moments, he glanced up at the ceiling as if to acknowledge his nana's role in this moment. A personal message she sent him in the form of a child in his lap.

I hear you, Nana, and I'll fix this place up. But I'm no father.

First thing they needed to do was get supplies. He hugged Gracie, then set her on the floor in front of him. "Thank you for my flowers. How about we go into town and get some stuff to fix this place up?"

Her little nose crinkled, so he added, "And ice cream?"

Juniper appeared in the doorway, but Gracie didn't give her time to say no. She flew past her mother and ran for her room. "Bag."

Juniper crossed her arms over her chest and sat on the edge of the couch facing him. "You play dirty. But we're not going into town with you."

She wasn't wrong; he knew better than to offer a kid ice cream to get what he wanted. Okay, he had a lot of work to do on himself, but one thing at a time. "Then you don't want to go into town to get an alarm system to install here and on the gates, so you'll know if a window or door opens when Gracie sees another bird to chase?"

A flash of relief crossed her face, but she buried it under her knitted brows. "That's a low-blow tactic."

"Just living up to your expectations of me." He winked, but he apparently had lost his charm because her lips didn't even twitch to prevent a smile. "You've changed." The words came out before he thought better of it.

"I grew up. I'm not a little girl that follows people blindly."

"Ouch. Got it." Hudson decided to try a new tactic. "Would you please go into town with me so that you can help pick out some tile for the kitchen, some supplies to make this farm a safer place for Gracie and to get some ice cream as a treat?"

"Fine, but I want—"

"Mint chocolate chip." It was his turn to smile. "Double scoop with cherries."

"You're not going to tell me that's gross?" Juniper's arms relaxed and her face didn't look so tense.

"Nope. I might even taste it."

Juniper's mouth fell open. "What happened to Hardnose Hudson?"

Nana's letter happened. "I sent him to one of my resorts on vacation while I work on the farm with you." He stood up and offered his hand. "Partners?"

"But we still don't know what we're going to do when we're done fixing up this place. We can't both live here." Her arms went back to crossed.

Feeling a little foolish standing with his hand outstretched, he dropped it to his side. "Maybe I'll come home on vacations or just own it from a distance. A silent partner. Let's make a deal—we'll work together until all the work is complete, and then we'll decide what to do with the farm. Maybe you'll decide this isn't the place for you after all and you'll let me buy you out at a higher price."

She rose and held out her hand. "Or you'll realize you've outgrown this place and leave it for Gracie and me to live."

They shook on it, but he knew there would be no way he'd ever agree to turn his nana's sacred place into some working farm with people trudging all around destroying the peace and quiet.

This was Nana's house and he'd protect it. It was all he could offer despite what his grandmother believed. She was wrong.

Hudson knew he was the wrong man for Juniper. He wasn't deserving of her and a little girl who could steal any man's heart no matter how cold or broken.

Chapter Five

Town gossip swirled around Juniper and Hudson with each step they took down Main Street. Gracie skipped along ahead of them, her purse swaying on her elbow and her hair bouncing. Juniper kept a good foot between her and Hudson as they walked side by side. Unfortunately, a crowd of people waiting outside Bless Your Heart Café drove them together. His fingers grazed hers, causing her breath to catch.

The door flew open, sending out the smell of deep-fried Southern favorites like chicken and french fries and okra.

"The letter I found from Nana said something strange I didn't understand." Hudson rubbed his forehead. He'd told her about the letter on the way into town.

"What?"

He let out a burst of air. "It said something about loss I don't even remember, but I remember my mom passing away. Every detail of it."

Her fingers slid in between his and she tugged

him around a family. "I'm sorry. I know that had to be traumatic, but I don't know what else she could mean." She eyed their fingers and quickly released him, shoving her hands into her pockets. A tingle remained behind that meandered up her arm.

Planters hung outside the shops with yellow and purple and pink flowers swaying in the gentle breeze, smacking the top of Hudson's head each time they walked under one.

"She said something before she passed about a box of important memories tucked away, but I don't know where or what."

"Strange." They walked a little farther without a word between them, and Juniper had a chance to catch her breath.

Gracie turned and pointed at the ice cream shop, standing on her toes but not quite as high as she normally did in crowds. She hadn't cried once either. Not even when the little boy bumped into her.

"We have to pick out tile first," Hudson said.

Juniper eyed Hudson with a raise of a brow. "I'm thinking dividing and conquering might be a better idea. She's going to get bored quick in the hardware store."

Hudson lit up like a billboard in New York City. "Leave that to me." He swooped Gracie up into his arms and flew her over his head like an airplane. "Do you want to travel on the express plane?"

Gracie squealed her delight. He swooped her up and down and into the hardware shop. Juniper gave him five minutes before he was ready to pull his hair out from Gracie acting up from the flickering lights and sounds and boredom.

The shop smelled of sawdust and paint fumes—a fact that didn't escape Gracie. "Icky." She pinched her nose and curled into herself. A good start to show Hudson he couldn't shuffle a kid around town, especially one with sensory issues.

He sat Gracie down on the ground and looked around the room, his attention settling on a display on an end cap while she rocked and held her nose and cried. "You like pink?"

She snapped her eyes open. "Uh-huh. Uh-huh." He took two bandannas off the display and unfolded them. "Let's pretend to be cowboys." He tied the black one over his nose behind his head and then held out the pink one. To Juniper's surprise, Gracie dropped her hands to her side and nodded.

Okay, so Hudson was resourceful. She didn't know he could be so creative, but she'd give him this one. The flickering light on the next aisle would be a bigger problem. Juniper knew this would be the end of his parenting skills.

Gracie cried and covered her eyes and crouched down in the corner. Hudson looked to Juniper.

"Told you, this isn't a good idea."

His lips curled into a mischievous grin, and he pulled his sunglasses out of his front pocket. "Every cowgirl needs sunglasses, right?"

He slid them over her eyes, and she popped up, her head moving left then right. She looked like an oversize, bank-robbing fly, but it worked.

"You coming? Tile's over here," he said in a triumphant tone.

Juniper followed Hudson with her mind still stuck on the image of him down on his knees tying bandannas and putting sunglasses on her daughter. All James ever did was ignore or yell at Gracie.

Hudson pointed to ultramodern long, thin gray tiles and announced, "This one. It's similar to the ones I put in our Caribbean resort last month. Guests love it."

"No." Juniper shook her head. "We're not refurbishing a resort hotel in the Caribbean, this is a farmhouse."

Gracie yanked off the bandanna and cried out, "Itchy."

He tilted his head, then eyed Gracie, then eyed the tile, then eyed Juniper. "Okay, what do you suggest?"

She pointed to the Southwestern-looking pattern.

Gracie took off the sunglasses and curled into Juniper, warning of an epic meltdown approaching. Hudson must've noticed it, too, because he bent over and tapped her nose, evoking a slight giggle and squirm.

"No." Hudson chuckled. "We don't live in the Wild West, we live in Georgia. Let's let Gracie choose."

While still curled into Juniper's leg, she stuck one finger out to a white subway tile in a pattern with a hint of gray flecks in it. Hudson tucked his hands in his pants pockets and rocked back on his heels, then squatted down to Gracie's height. "Are you an interior decorator? I might have to hire you to work for me."

Gracie giggled and smacked Hudson in the face with her palms, but instead of yelling at her for hitting him from her excitement, he kissed each palm and then lowered her hands.

He stood up in Juniper's space in the thin aisle. "What do you think?"

"I think you were smart to bring Gracie in here with us. I'm sold. It's a good compromise." Juniper's chest warmed at the sight of Gracie holding hands with Hudson. But that didn't make him a good father, and she needed to remember this was temporary.

A light flickered and a door squealed from the back of the shop. Too loud, too many stimuli.

Gracie squatted, covered her ears and turned

her head away from the light. Then let out a loud scream and rocked while humming.

Hudson looked to Juniper with wide eyes. He'd tried and had listened to what Juniper had told him about Gracie's challenges. And for a moment, she wanted to believe a man would stick around and try to help Gracie instead of judging her. A dangerous thought, so she decided to put a stop to their bonding and snagged Gracie up in her own arms. "Park and ice cream time?"

Hudson's eyebrow cocked with that knowing way of his, like he knew all her secrets without her sharing one.

"We'll let you check out. I'm going to take Gracie across to the park to play for a couple minutes. Wave us over when you're ready for ice cream."

Juniper bolted out of the store and across the street to a safe distance from Hudson. Gracie had come so far over the years. Juniper wouldn't let her guard down now. That man would forever break her heart, and she wouldn't let it happen again. No, she had to focus on her daughter, not on an old crush.

Children squealed and ran around the monkey bars. Mothers sat on the park bench knitting and chatting. The breeze brought the fragrance of fresh flowers and bacon from the café. Gracie took off running for the swings. "Push."

"I'm proud of you, Gracie. You did well in

the shop." Juniper pushed the swing and Gracie squealed with delight. "Hold tight."

Gracie held the chain so tight her fingers blanched. "What kind of ice cream do you want?"

She didn't answer. Instead, her eyes rolled back, and her head tilted to one side in pure delight, soothing the bad visual and auditory stimulation with physical movement.

Mindi walked over from the flower shop, waving madly. "Hey, squirrel. How's it going?"

Gracie didn't answer; she was too engrossed in her swinging. "Hi, Mindi. How was your date last night with Pastor John?"

She pressed a finger to her lips and looked around like a spy scanning for danger. "Shh, not so loud."

Juniper laughed. "You don't think the entire town knew the second you two sat down to eat?"

"No, we went north toward the city for a meal beyond town gossip."

Juniper didn't want to point out that probably half the town elders were watching out their windows and spotted them leaving town together.

"Why'd you do that if it was only a meeting about the event?"

A blush erupted on her pale cheeks. "Maybe it was a business date."

Hudson exited the clothing shop next to the café, but Ace Gatlin limped over, cornering him. The farm-fit man stood an inch taller than Hudson. His ex-football player physique had not changed since their high school days.

Mindi cleared her throat. "How's it going with Hudson?"

Gracie cried out, reminding Juniper to push again. "Fine. Just working to fix up the place." She eyed Ace and Hudson talking.

"What are you worried about? You think Ace is up to something?"

"No doubt hoping to strike a deal to buy the farm to expand the Gatlin name. That man has been a thorn in our backside since he inherited the place a few years ago."

"He doesn't talk much. I've tried to greet him, but he grunts and walks on. Rumor mill said he's been scarred from the war and I'm not talking about the one on his brow. I mean like in his heart and soul."

"I feel bad for him but that doesn't mean I want to sell him my land." Juniper thought about running over to warn Hudson of Ace's intentions, but she restrained herself.

"I wouldn't worry. Based on the legend of Hardnose Hudson, I'm guessing he can handle himself."

To her surprise, Hudson escaped in a matter of a minute and headed their way.

"Gotta run." Mindi made a quick escape as if

she didn't want to interrupt them from something. Hudson waved as he passed her, and she turned around and mouthed, "He's handsome. Go, girl."

Juniper ignored her and returned her attention to pushing the swing.

Hudson joined them. His lips pressed together as he eyed Gracie. "Someone's enjoying her swing."

Juniper felt defensive, knowing people judged her daughter as different. "The doctor explained that Gracie feels like she's flying all the time, that her stomach is always in her chest, and swinging and roller coasters and all things in motion calm her and she almost falls asleep."

"And she needed it after I dragged her into that hardware store." He toed the ground. "I get it. I love a good swing, too."

She longed to soothe that crinkle on his brow that always meant he felt like he'd done something wrong. "You did well. She's fine and you tried. That's more than her own father did."

"I'm sorry," he said but in a deep tone, like he meant more than just about the store incident.

He abandoned some bags of what appeared to be work clothes and sat on the swing by Gracie. He yelped and hollered, flying higher and higher, and Gracie shouted, "Mo. Mor. Mommy."

The two of them were quite the spectacle, drawing people from the café, hardware store, even the knitting shop. For once, Juniper saw the benefit of Hudson's superior attitude because he didn't care what people thought. A trait she had to admit shined as a plus for the man, but that didn't compensate for all the negatives.

"What did Ace want?" Juniper nudged.

"Not sure. He only said he was glad I was back." Hudson swung higher and poked Gracie in the side. "What happened to him anyway? He has a scar on his face and a limp, and his personality… I don't know, it's different from when we were in school together."

"Don't know, something happened in the military when he was serving." Juniper eyed the elderly women outside the knitting store. "Not even the Gossiping Grannies know."

Gracie's head rolled to the side, so Juniper stopped the swing before she fell off the seat. "Ready for ice cream?"

She shot off the swing and fell on her bottom, her head weaving around for a moment. A second later, she leaped up and took off running for the street.

"Halt!" Juniper shouted.

Gracie froze and held up one hand. Wow, she'd come a long way.

"You should be proud of her. She's a good kid," Hudson said and took one of Gracie's hands while Juniper took the other. They swung her up in the air and down, and for a moment, Juniper dared to imagine that her life could be this happy, but she knew better. She needed to remind Hudson and herself what they were supposed to be focused on.

"If I can get the hippotherapy program going, Gracie can find relief daily with the bouncing on the horse, not to mention increase of core muscle tone, fine motor coordination with holding the reins and—"

"I get it, but remember, we'll discuss our plans after the work is done. You might change your mind and use the money for multiple therapies and a good school."

"I'm not—"

"A day school. I'm not suggesting you send her away," he mouthed more than spoke, his face tight as if it pained him to even say the words.

For the briefest of moments, Juniper allowed herself to dream of a life like this one. The one with Hudson playing with Gracie, working the farm, and loving them both. But it was not even a dream, it was a fantasy. A fantasy that had already been proven impossible.

Hudson eyed his phone but still no messages or indication his father was in a hurry to reach him. Ace's interaction made him a little suspicious, but his father had always provoked paranoia in

Hudson, so he turned over the truck engine. The gray smoke rose from the tailpipe and the odor of gas reminded him of yesteryears. The truck had been around since he was a boy. Old and reliable, that was what Nana had called Beast. Juniper strapped Gracie in and before they made it to the edge of town, she fell asleep.

Juniper leaned her head back against the headrest and closed her eyes, taking in deep breaths. The poor woman ran so tight all the time. She reminded him of himself when he'd first started Kenworth Resorts with his partner, Mark Worthington. The thought of her dealing with so much stress stirred him inside.

He took the opportunity to steal a glance and enjoy the sunlight highlighting her tan skin and the way her long, thick lashes curled up. She'd always been a natural beauty. The kind of woman that never needed makeup or fancy clothes to be stunning. She looked more elegant in her royal blue collared shirt and khaki shorts than runway models did in heels and fancy gowns. James was a fool for hurting Juniper. Hudson wanted to hunt the man down and tell him he was stupid for letting this woman and Gracie slip from his life. Of course, Hudson had hurt her first.

"Stop staring and watch the road."

Hudson snapped his head back to center. "Just

checking to see if you were asleep. How'd you even know I was looking at you?"

"I could feel you staring."

He chuckled.

"What's so funny?"

"I forgot you had the eyes-in-the-back-of-your-head thing just like Nana did." He gripped the steering wheel, willing the pain of loss not to well up to the surface. It was one thing to grieve in private, but a man should never show emotions in public.

Juniper stretched and then turned her head, opening her eyes. "It's a mother thing, and with Gracie, I need eyes all over my head." She glanced over her shoulder as if to make sure her daughter hadn't broken free and run off.

He kept his gaze trained on the road ahead. For once in his life, he wasn't itching to get somewhere. "Well, hopefully the alarms will help. And I'll be around while we're fixing up the place."

Juniper huffed. "Let me be clear, Gracie is my responsibility. You're not her father."

An uncomfortable twinge in his chest made him adjust in his seat. "Harsh. You really don't think much of me, do you?"

She snickered, shook her head and crossed her arms over her chest in that way she did when she was shielding herself from a threat. "Haven't you preached to me since we were teenagers that you're heartless and heavy-handed like your father so I shouldn't want you in my life?"

She wasn't wrong. He had done that and much more. He'd done the wrong thing for the right reasons. Maybe if he hadn't pushed her so far out of his life, she wouldn't have ended up divorced with no money. "I did that to protect you."

"Yet now you want me to trust that you have a heart. I mean, I know you do, I'm just not sure it's connected to your brain. And you told me to leave the only real home I've had most of my life the minute you stepped on the property and discovered your nana had passed away."

Again, not wrong. He swallowed hard, that lump welled up so high in his throat it threatened tears in his eyes. He turned off Main Street onto the road toward the farm and watched the tall grass pass by. "You remember when we were young, and we'd play hide-and-seek in that field?"

She tapped her fingernail against the window and a smile tugged the corner of her lips. "It was more hide-and-scare. I'd remain so still that once a grasshopper landed on my cheek and I didn't even scream." Her laughter filled the car with such joy.

Her smile warmed his insides as if the sun could penetrate his skin. He didn't like that Juniper hadn't smiled since he'd arrived, and he knew he'd been a big cause of that. Not because of setting her up with James but because he'd turned her away any time she'd needed a friend. Not because he didn't care but because he'd cared too much. He wanted to see her sunshine break through the dark clouds of her last few years, and helping her relax and not worry so much would be a good start.

"We were children then, though." Juniper sat up and straightened her button-down shirt.

"I'm sorry. Listen, relax. Think about it this way. I've always been honest. All these years, I've warned you to stay away, so if I tell you that you can trust me then you should believe me, right?"

"I guess so." She rested her hands in her lap and studied her nails.

"I vow not to pull any stunts or try to make you leave. And I promise to finish the renovations before I return to work and that I won't run off without a word. And you promise to relax a little." He offered his hand.

She didn't move for several seconds. That was the second time she'd left him hanging, and he didn't like it. People shook hands during a business deal. "Hello?"

"Fine, I agree." She shook his hand but withdrew before he could register her touch.

He didn't like it. She'd always pursued him, and he'd always been the one to pull away. Not that it mattered; nothing had changed. Juniper deserved a good man in her life and so did Gracie. They needed a man who would be soft-spoken, generous and kind. Hudson knew how to take what he wanted, make money and work hard. Not good qualities for a husband or father.

The turn to the long drive didn't come soon enough, because the longer he sat in the car with Juniper, the more his imagination took him on a drive into what-if land. What if he had married Juniper instead of setting her up with James? What if he'd been here before Nana passed away? What if he'd stayed in touch with James?

"What are you torturing yourself about over there? You've got that pinched brow and I-wish-I-could-but-I-can't look on your face."

He pulled the truck to a stop in front of the house and swung open his door to escape the conversation and his runaway thoughts. It had to be nostalgia. His return home had stirred up old feelings that didn't matter anymore. "I'm thinking we best get to work." He snagged the groceries and carried them to the kitchen while Juniper retrieved Gracie.

"I see you still use your go-to move of running away when things stir up feelings. That ugly word in your emotional dictionary."

A bird perched on the front porch gutter chirped its agreement.

"It's already getting late, and I'd like to get the sensors and alarm installed in the house before Gracie goes to bed tonight." Hudson went to work with the sound of *Little Einsteins* in the background. It took him all afternoon and well into the evening, but he had sensors on every window and door in the house and the alarm set up.

Juniper came out wearing an apron, wiping her hands on a towel. "I'm impressed. I figured you'd hire someone to do any manual labor around here."

He wiped off his papa's old tools and placed them neatly into the toolbox before he stood and stretched the kinks from his back. "When I first started Kenworth Resorts, who do you think did all the restorations?"

She raised a brow at him. "Really?"

"I didn't have any capital. My buddy Mark and I started off with a small hotel on the main island and worked for an entire year. We ate fish we caught and white rice, saving every penny we could to restore the old place, then we sold it."

"I thought you bought and ran hotels?" Juniper squatted by Gracie. "Hon, you have three minutes, then it's time to wash up for dinner."

"Yes, well, with the capital of the first hotel, we invested in a second, and when we were done, we decided to keep it and hire a management company to run it. Now we've expanded into fourteen hotels. The last one was a massive multimillion-dollar renovation and we have it up and running."

"Impressive."

All the awards he'd won, all the accolades and money he'd earned, none of it warmed his chest more than that one word from Juniper. "It's not like I'm the CEO of the largest company in the nation or anything, but I've done okay."

"Stop that," Juniper scolded in the reprimanding tone he'd heard her use on Gracie a couple of times.

"Stop what?"

She threw her hands up in the air, sending the towel into a wave. "Stop comparing yourself to that sorry excuse for a father of yours. Be proud of who you are. You did it, you made it. When are you going to enjoy all that money you worked so hard to get?"

"It's not that simple."

"Two minutes, Gracie." Juniper about-faced with some remark under her breath.

"What's that?"

"I said, when are you going to realize that there is never enough money? James and I had plenty for a while, but it didn't make us happy."

"I'm sorry about what happened. Listen, I can help. I've got a lot of money tied up right now, but I can lend you money for Gracie's therapy."

"I don't want your money. Besides, I'd never

be able to pay it back." She eyed the iPad, then her watch.

"Then I'll give it to you. How much do you need? I'll transfer the money to your account now." He yanked his phone from his pocket.

"I'm not going to let you buy me out, so stop trying. This fight is about more than money."

"I didn't say that I'd buy you out. I already told you we'll fix this place up together and then we'll decide what to do."

She crossed her arms over her chest and eyed Gracie. "One minute."

"Take the money, Juniper. Don't be stubborn." Hudson entered his code and pulled up his banking app.

"Thirty seconds."

Gracie let out a groan.

Juniper rounded on Hudson with a narrow-eyed gaze. "I don't need nor want your money. Didn't you hear me? Money doesn't buy happiness. When are you going to see that? It never bought your father happiness, and you said how you didn't want to be like him, but that is who you've become. You can't buy forgiveness either."

Her words drilled an arrow of regrets through his heart. "That's not fair. I'm not my father. If I was my father, I would've taken everything I wanted without considering the consequences."

"And what did you want, Hudson? What is it that you sacrificed?"

He wanted to tell her, but the words were locked so deep inside him under all the other wishes and torments of his past, he couldn't find the right ones to say.

Juniper walked over and knelt next to Gracie. "Time's up, hand over the iPad."

"No." Gracie cuddled it to her chest and Hudson felt a meltdown coming on.

He wanted to intervene and help, but after his failure at the hardware store and now his mind swooshing and swishing with so many thoughts, he stayed out of it. And the answer came to him. He wanted Juniper. More than anything in life, he wanted to marry her and love her, but he couldn't. He'd done what his father never could—sacrificed his own wishes to protect the woman he loved.

Gracie rolled, putting her body over the iPad to keep it. "No! No! No!"

He couldn't speak. He couldn't say what he wanted. Not aloud, and not to Juniper, because it didn't matter. Even today, he wasn't the man Juniper needed. She needed a father for her child and a man who wanted to remain on this farm and raise children and live a simple life. She wanted too much. He wouldn't be his father, but he couldn't be the man she needed either.

Chapter Six

The morning sun streaked bright light through Juniper's room. She flew out of bed and spotted the time as 8:30. Before she even pulled on a robe, she raced to Gracie's room, but she wasn't there.

Juniper's heart pounded with terror but then she remembered the alarm system had been installed. Still, it was unnervingly quiet. At the end of the hall, she spotted Gracie on a chair by the door, standing on her tiptoes to reach the new lock that Hudson had installed.

That was why Juniper had slept so well. The idea that she didn't have to keep one eye open to make sure Gracie didn't escape was a blessing like none she'd been given in years. Since Nana had gotten too sick to watch Gracie while Juniper took naps, she'd barely slept.

At the sight of Gracie, calmness soothed her anxiety. She took a deep breath and went up behind Gracie quietly. "Excuse me, young lady. What're you doing?"

Gracie spun too fast and fell from the chair,

but Juniper caught her before she hit the floor. "This is why we don't climb chairs."

"I please?" Gracie clasped her hands under her chin and raised her shoulders.

"No iPad for today. You disobeyed the rules last night. I gave you the countdown, so you need to hand it to me once the countdown is done. That's what we agreed to, and you don't want to break a promise. That isn't good."

Gracie shoved her hands into her lap and made her I'm-not-happy face—chin to chest, looking up so high her pupils disappeared. "Hud?"

"Who?"

"There." Gracie pointed out the window, so Juniper stood and peered outside to find Hudson moving wood from the truck to the corral.

So much for the man who'd worked his way up to ordering others to do manual labor. Sure, he'd installed the alarm yesterday, but this was hard physical labor. Maybe he'd changed. The loss of a loved one could have a profound impact on someone. Maybe she'd been too judgmental. After all, because of him, she'd slept all night. "Gracie, you can watch thirty minutes of *Little Einsteins* but then we'll have to get some breakfast and go to work. I'm going to change and help Hudson for a few minutes."

Gracie ran over and plopped down in front of the television and Juniper flipped it on, changed her clothes, entered the alarm code the way Hudson had shown her, then went outside.

Sweat poured down Hudson's brow. He lifted a board up, slung it over his shoulder and dropped it into the pile. His muscles strained against his drenched T-shirt, and if Juniper didn't know better, she'd think he'd worked on the farm all his life.

Hummingbirds fluttered in her belly at the sight of the man who would never be hers. She knew she had been burned by the eighteen-year-old who'd run away. No, she needed to let go of the hate and work on herself the way the Bible told her to—by letting go of the past resentment—so she marched up to him.

He removed his bandanna and wiped his brow. Before she thought better of it, she stood on her tiptoes and planted a kiss on his dirty cheek.

He froze midswipe.

"It's a thank-you." If she didn't know better, she'd think Hudson blushed.

"I don't know what I did, but I hope you tell me so I can do it again."

A pull to kiss him again made her take a step back. His strong frame and protective nature still drew her in with a false promise that he'd be there when she needed him most. "Last night was the first night in ages I've slept. Thanks to that alarm,

I didn't have to worry about Gracie escaping and getting hurt."

He removed his gloves and tossed them in the back of the truck. "I'm glad I could help. As I said, I'm here to work with you, not against you."

She studied the wood chips on the ground as if they were the pieces of his heart that had flaked off over the years. "Maybe."

A bird squawked overhead, and he studied it for a minute then moved in close to her, too close. He captured her gaze with soft but firm eyes. "You can trust me. Like I told you, I've never lied to you. I might not have been the man you wanted me to be, but I've always been honest."

She couldn't argue with him on that point. He'd been honest when he showed up with a bag in hand and announced he was leaving, fifteen years ago. "Guess after being married to a gambling addict, I've developed some trust issues." She eyed the house and knew she needed to return to Gracie before her show was over. "Breakfast?"

"I'd like that, thanks." Hudson eyed the woodpile. "I need to finish this first, then I'll get cleaned up. Shouldn't take more than twenty minutes."

"I'd help, but I can't change Gracie's morning routine. Like I told you, she doesn't deal well with change."

Hudson nodded. "And she's had to deal with a lot of change in recent months."

A shadow passed over his expression.

The pain etched in the unfamiliar lines around his eyes. She couldn't help but put a hand on his arm for comfort. "I know, I miss her, too."

"You're still the same person, full of comfort and kindness." He adjusted his gloves. A long breath escaped his lungs. "Yet, you're a different person now. I left so you could stay, my sweet June Bug, I mean Juniper, but another man took your innocence and let you down."

"No, I grew up and I'm stronger for it." She backstepped, worrying for Gracie's safety. "And I'm not sorry because God gave me that beautiful and sweet little girl in there."

Hudson quirked a brow. "You're still all sunshine to my grump, aren't you?"

"I don't know. I think we've both changed. Now, get back to work, cowboy. You need to earn your keep." She winked and about-faced to march back to the safety of her home, far from thoughts of Hudson and believing he could be her savior. She'd learned long ago, the only savior in her life was Jesus.

Gracie still sat in front of *Little Einsteins*, her hair swishing back and forth as she moved her body to the music. Juniper hurried to pull out all the ingredients to make pancakes. With Hudson here to help with some of the work, she focused on some therapeutic exercises to keep Gracie from regressing any further. Perhaps, someday, she'd be able to turn this place into more than just hippotherapy. There could be occupational, physical and speech therapists to work with children.

The final song ended, and Gracie padded into the kitchen. "Pa-cakes?"

"Only if you help make them." Juniper held her breath waiting for her to refuse, but armed with a good night's sleep, Juniper was ready for the battle.

"Hud eat?" Gracie bounced onto her tiptoes, her big blue eyes shining with hope.

"Yes, he'll join us." Juniper pointed to all the ingredients spread out on the table. They'd be making pancakes from scratch today. A messy activity with Gracie's help but it would be great to work on her fine motor skills, counting, speech, grip strength and focus.

Gracie went to the apron drawer and pulled one out, slid it over her head, then ran to Juniper to get it tied. But Juniper remembered what the therapist said about fine motor skills, so she wrapped the strings around her middle to the front. "You tie."

A whimper sounded from Gracie, but Juniper knelt down and took her hands the way Hudson had the other morning. "I'll help."

Even with guiding Gracie, her little muscles tensed. Juniper helped hold the string to flip it over, then held up a bow and wrapped it around. And then, once Gracie had bows looped together, Juniper let go. “Okay, now pull slowly.”

Gracie tugged them until it formed a bow. She gasped and held her hands to her lips. The front door opened, and Hudson walked inside. “Wow, look at Gracie. She’s growing up.”

A smile beamed from ear to ear on her daughter. Juniper knew to most people this would be a tiny accomplishment, but to her, this opened a door to the rest of the world. It proved she could do anything if given a little patience and time.

“I’m going to go shower if that’s okay, and then I’ll come back to help.”

“No. I do.” Gracie climbed up onto her special chair and pulled the flour to her, dumping some onto the table. She gasped and waited. James would’ve yelled at her, but Hudson swooped in, picked up a pinch and made it snow over her head.

Her giggles filled the room and Juniper’s heart. Why couldn’t Hudson see all these years of fearing himself to be his father had no merit? Because he’d make the most amazing father. Not for Gracie, but for some child someday.

“I’m looking forward to Gracie’s pancakes. My

stomach's already growling." He rubbed his belly and backed out of the room.

The water cut on down the hallway and Gracie patted Juniper's belly. "Mommy. Help."

"Right, um, okay. Let's start measuring the ingredients." Pride didn't begin to describe how Juniper felt watching her daughter work hard using her hands. Only once did she have an almost meltdown, but when Hudson came in with damp hair and that sweet smile, she took a deep breath and went back to work.

When the pancakes were finally mixed, Gracie fell over exhausted, covered her ears and went to her room.

Hudson smelled of fresh spring. His damp hair fell over his brow in a casual way that made him look less formal and stuffy and more…inviting. He grabbed a rag. "She okay?"

Juniper shook off her thoughts. "Yes, too much stimuli and stress, but she did great."

"That she did." Hudson wiped down the table. "Looks like when we tried to make a birthday cake for Nana. You remember that?"

"Ha, of course I do." Juniper poured some batter into the frying pan. "Nana said it looked like we'd had a food fight." She eyed the flour on the floor and countertop. Perhaps it was because she'd had so much rest and felt secure that Gracie couldn't leave the house with the alarm and locks, but for the first time in years, a spark of playfulness took hold. She took a handful of flour and tossed it at a clean Hudson.

"Hey, what was that for?" He picked up his own handful and tossed it back at her.

Before they knew it, they were slipping and sliding and clinging to each other to remain standing on a slick floor of baking ingredients.

They fell into the wall laughing, holding on to each other. The pancake aroma reminded her she had to get back to the stove, but when he cupped her cheek, she forgot all about the food. Her pulse quickened.

A knock at the front door drew him away at just the right moment before she got lost in nostalgic thoughts of Hudson again.

"I'll go see who that is." He cleared his throat, slipped away and went to the door, allowing Juniper to breathe and think once more.

With the distance, she realized this was a mistake, letting Hudson into her life. But maybe he had changed. He certainly showed a softer side than he had in years. Could there be something there?

She plated the pancakes, turned off the stove and went to the window where she heard voices outside. She peered through the curtain to discover Ace talking with Hudson in what appeared to be an intense conversation.

There was no doubt what Ace wanted, but why would he be talking to Hudson again? She opened the window, cringing at the alarm's short beep, hoping it wouldn't set Gracie off, not to mention the possibility of Hudson hearing it from across the lawn. When he didn't look over, and Gracie didn't erupt, Juniper listened.

"I'll buy the land for a reasonable price, and you can come visit whenever you want."

Hudson scrubbed his stubble-covered jaw. "Listen, I'll consider your proposal and let you know."

She wouldn't have believed it if she hadn't heard the truth with her own ears. The man who'd just spouted promises of honesty was already betraying her.

Hudson closed the tailgate on the truck and eyed the work he'd completed so far today. He'd missed working with his hands instead of sitting behind a desk all day. Maybe his father was right, and he didn't have a brain.

No, he'd proven that man wrong. A man who hated himself for making the wrong decision in his life. Had Hudson avoided the same decision for the right reasons?

Ace walked around the truck and eyed the land. Hudson knew that look. It was the look of a man who wanted what he couldn't have. "Now, come on. You and I both know your nana couldn't keep up with this place, and it's gone downhill, yet I'm ready to make a generous offer. I don't want this place going to some secret corporation or something. Let's keep it in the Willow Oaks family."

Hudson's warning bells went off like there was a ten-alarm fire. Could his father be using Ace as a frontman? "As I said, I'll think about it." He had no intention of thinking about it, but he wanted to know more information. "What land's been bought? Is it one company or several that purchased land near Willow Oaks?"

"Think it's one company based on what my buddy told me. Says it's been all quiet like and slow."

"We'll talk more soon. I need to get back inside for now."

They shook as neighbors did but with an undertone of control in Ace's grip. "What will it take? Name it."

Hudson wanted to ask him what the jagged scar along his temple and his limp were from but considered it rude. The man looked damaged, not just on the surface but behind his eyes. Like he carried baggage so heavy he'd never be able to walk straight again.

Juniper swung open the front screen door, which slammed against the side of the house, and hotfooted up to the side of his truck with fire in her eyes. Hudson knew that look, but he didn't know why she wanted to run him out of town.

"This is my land, and I'm not selling, so you can get off my property now, Ace. We've been through this, and you know my answer."

"Your land? Hudson Kenmore is Mrs. Kenmore's grandson, so I think it's his choice or his father's."

"What about my father?" Hudson stepped forward. "Have you been talking to him? He ask you to make an offer for this property?"

"No. I wouldn't do that. We were friends once, so I know all about your old man."

"Doesn't matter. The land's not for sale." Juniper rounded on Hudson.

"I didn't agree to anything. Just listened to the man," Hudson protested, but based on her narrow-eyed, I'm-never-going-to-trust-you-again glower, he knew it would be pointless at the moment to try to explain.

"Nana left the house to me, so it's my land. We had plans, and, in her name, I'm going to see them through." Juniper fisted her tiny hands ready to fight the world, so he knew she wouldn't listen to a word anyone else had to say on the matter.

"A horse program for handicapped kids? Stupid idea. No way it'll keep this farm alive. Sell to me and you and your handicapped daughter can live somewhere better for you both. This land is hard work."

Hudson's hackles rose at the way he referred to Gracie. "I think it's best you go. And for your information, people don't use the term *handicapped* anymore."

"Yeah, they do. I've been called that plenty." He knocked on his leg and it echoed, indicating his gait was from a prosthetic leg. "Fine, but I'm going to take a look at that will once it's filed at the courthouse. I doubt it's legal." Ace slithered back to his truck, leaving a bad taste in Hudson's mouth and a fire in his belly to make sure his family farm was safe from Ace and any corporation.

Hudson turned to Juniper, his temper still flaring at Ace. "I told you I'd never do something behind your back. I've done a lot wrong, but unlike my father, my word has always meant something."

"That man is not an option. Do you understand me?" Juniper said, restrained and bitter.

"As I said, I didn't make any deals, but I wanted to keep dialogue open because he has information about land being sold in the county. And I won't lose my nana's home when I can save it. Not after all the years she spent keeping this place running despite my father hounding her to sell. I'm going to send the will to my lawyer and make sure he can't take this place."

"You really think he'll try?"

"I do. If he still wants to demolish it like he vowed when I was younger."

Juniper closed her eyes and shook her head.

"Leave it to me. Business dealings are my specialty. I'm going to dig into this further so I can keep this place safe from being gobbled up for some underhanded road deal to a shopping mall."

"That's your problem, isn't it, Hudson Kenmore? You're always trying to save people from themselves. Well, who's going to save you from yourself?" She about-faced, took three steps, then rounded on him again. If he wasn't irritated himself, he might notice how cute she was when her hair fell free around her shoulders and her nose crinkled.

"Maybe in your high and mighty world, you string people along and play dangerous games, but this place is my heart, and that man can't have it. Ace tried to drive Nana out of here when times were tough, so yes, there's a reason to shut him down. That deal is never going to happen, so you listen to me." She marched up and poked her finger into his chest. "I'd never let Nana down like that." She turned on her heels and stormed up the front porch steps, swung open the door and yelled over her shoulder. "And if you ever cared about her then you'd never entertain Ace's offer again."

Hudson cringed at her words. Nana would trump everything. That was why he had stayed. To pay an old debt. Not to mention his partner had guilted him into it. How could he not look into what was going on around them? He'd seen many small resorts circle the whirlpool of heartfelt bad decisions only to be sucked down into the dark abyss of debt and bankruptcy.

He decided not to try to explain that to Juniper and instead give her some space to cool off, so he went to his apartment and decided to check in on Mark. The phone only rang twice before his partner picked up. "No, you haven't been there long enough, and you're not coming back for some big business deal you found."

Hudson huffed. "Why does everyone think I'm going to run away before my work is done here?"

"Sorry, man. Just figured." Mark coughed and hacked.

"How are you doing?"

"Still living."

"Not funny." Hudson rubbed his forehead. "Maybe I should head back."

"Oh no, you're not using me as your escape excuse. What did you call for? I'm sure there's a reason."

He cringed at the fact that Mark wasn't wrong.

"I'm looking into who is buying up land in the county. If I send you details, can you have our guy dig deep and find out what corporation is snagging up land cheaply?"

"You think it's your father?"

Hudson's blood simmered. "Hope not, but I'm going to send Nana's will to our lawyer."

His phone chimed and he read the text real quick.

Gracie's upset she made Hudcakes and Hud's not here.

He put the cell back to his ear. "Gotta run, but I'm going to call you once a week to check on you."

"You mean to find out if there's any new business you can work on?"

"No, I mean it. To check on you. You might be the only pseudo-family I have left in this world that I actually like." Before Mark said something sappy or snappy, Hudson ended the call and raced down the rickety stairs, his heart tight with worry that he'd caused Gracie a meltdown. Funny, he'd avoided kids in restaurants and shopping and anywhere else that children went. Their tantrums always gave him a headache or made him uncomfortable. Outward emotions of any kind made him uncomfortable. It was how he knew for sure he'd never make a good father. But for some reason, Gracie didn't make him want to run away but toward her.

Maybe it was because she had to work so hard for everything and small wins were cause for major celebration. He admired hard work and determination. That little girl made him feel alive and needed for the first time in his life, and he wanted to see her succeed.

To his relief, he found Gracie standing with a plate in her two hands, holding it up to him. "Hudcakes."

His world shone bright all around him from Gracie's big smile, and the hope in her eyes made him want to give that little girl the world. "Thank you. This looks delicious." He took the plate and sat down at the table next to Juniper.

She side-whispered, "Sorry, but it meant a lot for you to eat her pancakes."

"It means a lot she made them for me."

Gracie sat with her hands in prayer under her chin, watching him like she did hummingbirds. He didn't care if the pancakes tasted like cow manure, he'd choke down every last bite for her. With his breath held in case he needed to hide his dislike, he cut a small piece and put it in his mouth. To his surprise, buttery, homemade goodness exploded on his tongue. "Wow." He dug in and took another massive bite. The aroma took him back to childhood. "A hint of cinnamon? Vanilla? And Nana's special secret ingredient?"

"Uh-huh. Uh-huh." Gracie bounced on her knees and clapped. "Like?"

"Like them?" He choked down an unexpected surge of emotions and scooped Gracie into his arms. "Love them. You must be one special little girl to be allowed to make Nana's secret pancakes."

"Hudcakes." Gracie's little arms wrapped around his neck, and she squeezed out any bit of grayness from his world. She didn't let go for several seconds, and a lump lodged in his throat.

"You brought me a touch of Nana. Thank you." His voice cracked. "It's been a long time since I felt this kind of love."

"Okay, time to eat. Show Hudson how you can feed yourself with your special fork without any help."

Gracie crawled back into her seat, picked up her fork with two hands, her tongue out to one side with her lips closed, which he realized was her deep concentration face. She stabbed the already-cut pancakes like a spear to a wild fish in the river. With extreme focus, she lifted the fork, leaned down with her head sideways and plunged the pancake into her mouth, dropped her fork and placed her hands over her lips with a squeal.

"Good job, honey." Juniper dabbed at her eyes

and Hudson had a sudden urge to pull them both in for a celebratory hug, but the way Juniper shot up from her seat and adjusted Gracie in the chair, then poured milk and put some ingredients away told him she still needed space. A ravine of space at the moment. And he didn't like it.

He didn't like it one bit.

Chapter Seven

The evening light faded, and Gracie turned off the television all on her own and ran to her room.

Hudson leaned back on the couch and stretched his arms over his head. "She hasn't had any sort of issue in a week."

Juniper fought the fear rising up inside her. "Routine. She's all about schedules and order. When her life changes, she faces too much for her to handle. After the divorce, she regressed in speech and behavior. Nana helped, but when she got too sick to get out of bed for the last few months, Gracie regressed again. She needs stability and strict schedules."

"She's doing great. You should be proud of her—and you." Hudson's eyes shone with something new in the dim light from the old fringe lamp on the side table. His face wasn't tight and stressed. A tan had kissed his skin after only two weeks of hard farm labor. He looked good. Too good.

To her surprise, he had worked sunup to sundown and not one crew showed up to do the labor. "You should be proud of yourself, too."

He shifted to face her. With one knee casually up on the couch, he looked relaxed and calm. Nothing like the Hudson she'd known in the last decade or so. "What for?"

"You've been working hard."

He laughed. "You thought I was all board-rooms and personal trainers, someone who'd never get his hands dirty."

She shrugged. "Maybe."

"I told you I did all the renovations to the first couple hotels, but it's fine. I don't blame you for thinking that about me."

Gracie toe-ran to the couch and climbed up with the illustrated hardback book *The Little Drummer Boy*, which hadn't made an appear-ance in a long time. It was a sign of healing.

Juniper leaned back so Gracie couldn't see her lips and mouthed to Hudson, "Nana's book. Hasn't pulled it out since she fell too ill to read."

Hudson nodded acknowledgment that he un-derstood this was a big moment showing how Gracie was starting to heal from the loss. "Hud read?" She shoved the corner of the book into Hudson's broad chest, not allowing him a chance to say no.

Juniper smiled and leaned back again, her eyes heavy from hard work and caring for Gracie. And thanks to Hudson, she'd been able to relax a little, not having to worry about Gracie escaping from the house or the barn or the corral. The man had Gracie-proofed most of the farm. She believed he would've Gracie-proofed the world if he could. If only her own father had put that much into keeping her safe.

Hudson's soft, deep voice read the words of the Christmas story that brought so much hope into the world. Juniper knew why Nana and Gracie loved it so much. Juniper could never make it through reading it aloud without getting choked up.

The words faded and she relaxed into the corner of the couch knowing Gracie couldn't be any safer than in Hudson's arms. A thought that would terrify her if she wasn't so comfortable. His voice faded and dreams came in the form of hippotherapy and a barn wedding. She jolted upright to find herself covered by a blanket, with Gracie standing over her holding her stuffed bear tight, morning light pouring into the living room.

Gracie patted Juniper on the face. "Hudcakes?"

"Sure." Juniper wiped the sleep from her eyes and heard the sound of a hammer, indicating Hudson was already hard at work. "Let's go help Hud for a bit, then we'll get breakfast on. Can you be a big girl and press the coffee button while I change?"

"Uh-huh, uh-huh." Gracie padded off and Juniper dressed. Then Juniper grabbed two mugs and made her way out to the barn, where she found Hudson working on the horse stalls.

"Brought you some coffee."

Gracie ran past and wrapped her arms around Hudson's thigh. "Morn, Hud."

"Morning, Sweet Gracie Girl." He swung her up into the air, then hugged her tight and set her back on her feet.

"I get eggs." She stumbled in her galoshes but recovered.

Juniper moved to the back window so she could keep an eye on Gracie despite the gate alarm.

Hudson tossed his tools into the toolbox and grasped the cup as if it held the elixir of life. "Thank you. I needed this."

"Welcome." Juniper eyed the repaired boards on the ceiling, the reinforced stairs, the stall door repairs. "You've been busy."

He shrugged. "Someone had to get to work since someone else needed her beauty sleep. Well, not that you need it. I mean, you're already beautiful, but, well, ah, you know what I mean." He toed the dirt with his new, already dirty boots and took a big gulp of his coffee, hiding behind the mug.

She chuckled. It had been a long time since

she'd seen Hudson tongue-tied. Memories flooded in at the sight of the hayloft and she remembered the last time he'd ever sounded so nervous. A blush rushed up from her chest to her neck to her face.

The kiss. A knee-weakening, promise-to-love-you-forever kiss. A lie kiss.

She shook off the memory and retreated to the chicken coop with Gracie picking flowers along the edge of the fence line. Today, the barn and fencing and chicken coop would be complete, and it would be time to start on the kitchen renovations. Not that the house needed any work besides some repairs, but Hudson insisted. She didn't want too much to change, though, because she clung to their childhood. If only Hudson could remember the good times.

They'd spent summer days chasing each other through fields and winter nights by the fire sipping hot cocoa and playing games. Those were some of her fondest memories in her life, before Hudson's father finally got his way and Hudson left for good.

With the last chicken wire secured, she decided to make some Hudcakes with Gracie—not that she wanted pancakes again, but the repetitiveness they'd been living with had gone a long way for Gracie. Juniper would choke down all the Hudcakes she could manage if it meant stability for her sweet girl.

"Gracie, let's go make breakfast."

No answer.

Juniper's rapid pulse sent a surge of adrenaline through her body. She ran to the edge of the barn, but Gracie wasn't picking wildflowers anymore.

Her breath came in short bursts, her gaze darted from one fence post to the next and stars burst in her vision. No sign of Gracie doing anything inside the corral anymore. But the gate door still remained latched and none of the new chicken wire they'd installed was peeled back for her to escape.

Juniper managed to take in a deep breath and stomp down the panic rising up but then realized a fence alone couldn't keep her flying squirrel inside. If Gracie wanted to get out, she'd find a way. She'd gotten complacent with the faux sense of security.

Juniper had become too relaxed, relying too much on Hudson playing the part of a father. But he wasn't Gracie's father. He was a man who would be gone once they finished the renovations.

Terror zipped through her, sending her into a sprint to the other side of the barn where she scanned the tree line but found no sign of her. "Gracie!" she screamed.

No time for pride. She raced into the barn to get Hudson. Her pulse pounded a fast and hard tempo. She stumbled over Hudson's toolbox and fell into one of the stall doors. Breathless, she looked up to find Gracie snuggled in Hudson's lap in a pile of hay holding wildflowers.

Gracie laughed and bounced and looked happy.

But instead of Juniper's pulse slowing, her heart bounded so hard it felt like it would burst because she saw the truth.

This wasn't about an old flame who stirred Juniper up and made her believe in possibilities again. No, this was far worse. Gracie believed he'd be sticking around—but he wouldn't.

In a matter of days or weeks or months, Hudson would be gone, and Gracie would lose one more person she loved, causing her to regress again. This time, Juniper wasn't sure she'd ever recover.

No, she wouldn't allow it. She marched up to the hay. "Gracie, change of plans. We're going into town. I need to check on something."

"Hudcakes," she said, then jutted out her lip into a pouty face.

"Ice cream?" Juniper resorted to the one thing she scolded Hudson about, but now wasn't the time to worry about good parenting; this was a time to worry about protecting her child.

Gracie gasped. "I-ceam. Yes." She shot out of Hudson's lap and ran out of the barn.

Juniper turned on Hudson.

He lifted up his hands, one holding the purple wildflowers Gracie had given him. "Oh no, what did I do now? You've got the arms crossed, and the I'm-going-to-let-you-have-it face."

She dropped her arms but kept her focus on what was important. Gracie.

"You need to stay away from my daughter. You're confusing her, and when you leave, it's going to crush her."

The beautiful spring afternoon felt bitter and cold with the rain drizzling and the cloud coverage. Hudson finished working in the barn, walked the property, and did some measuring and online shopping for some supplies since he thought it best to remain on the farm and not run into Juniper in town.

Instead, he sat at Nana's desk and held her Bible in his hands. The fading light reflected off the gold-embossed lettering as if highlighting his need to open the book.

He'd given up religion years ago. The moment he walked away from the farm, he knew he'd be on his own. He couldn't ask God to help him if he'd chosen money over family, and he'd done it all himself. Proving his father wrong.

He didn't need anyone, not even God, to succeed in life. His father had always preached that only weak people needed religion.

Then why did he feel so empty inside? He hadn't realized until Juniper and Gracie left for town how much they'd filled that vacant space inside him. A space he realized wasn't from Nana's passing, although that hurt to his core. But he'd had that space inside him since the day he'd left the farm.

He ran his fingers over the gold letters. His mother had once told him all the answers were inside the good book, but what had her faith ever gotten her but a cheating husband who abandoned her when she needed him most? She died before she'd had a chance to live.

Tears welled up, but he forced them away and opened the book, facing the words that promised so much but didn't deliver.

Where was God when his mother died of a broken heart at such a young age?

He closed the book and tossed it onto the desk. No, God hadn't been there then, and He wouldn't care about this now. Hudson needed to see this through and help Juniper even if she didn't want his money or assistance.

The sun dipped lower, so Hudson stood up, peering between the front lace curtains to see if he could spot the old truck heading home. Certainly they'd be home by dinner. If not, he could use the car he'd extended the rental on.

He opened his laptop and plopped down on the couch where he'd read to Gracie and tucked Juniper in for the night. His heart had been full then.

With a deep breath, he pushed his wayward thoughts away and studied the email the lawyer had sent. Not what he'd hoped but what he'd expected. His father could contest it if he wanted with his team of high-priced lawyers who always won their cases.

There was nothing he could do about that except hope his father didn't know about Nana's passing, so he searched through the documents his business associate had sent. After an hour of sifting through the zoning maps and property sales and identifying that they were all bought by shell companies, he saw it. His father's footprint. But why? The sales dated back over a decade. If it was his father, why didn't he ever develop the land?

None of it made sense.

Crunching gravel drew him to the window, but to his disappointment, it wasn't Juniper. It was Ace Gatlin. Great, what was he doing here again?

Hudson made his way outside hoping to get him to leave before Juniper came home and saw him here and made the assumption that Hudson was working behind her back.

Ace hopped dov
a container of som
Made some of my
ies and thought I'd

“Thank you.” Hudson took the
like they were a sugary bribe. He had no choice
but to accept it, though, if he wanted him to leave
quickly. “I appreciate you coming by. I've got to
get back to work, though.”

“I'll be on my way, but we need to get together
and talk about my offer.” He passed the cookies
but didn't let them go. “Don't let Juniper discourage you from what you know is best for everyone. I know she can bat her eyelashes and make
your good judgment get cloudy.”

Hudson didn't like the way he spoke about Juniper. He straightened to match Ace's height. “I
can assure you that no woman has ever dissuaded
me from the appropriate business decision. I base
my decisions on numbers and facts. And the fact
is that there is a good reason for me to keep this
property.”

As if God was trying to teach him a lesson,
a truck turned onto the main drive and barreled
down on them.

“I think it's best you leave.” Hudson thought
about pushing the cookies back at the man, but
Nana would scold him for being rude.

The truck slid to a stop, spitting rocks and dust

Ace hopped down out of his truck and held a container of something. "Hi, there, Hudson. Made some of my grandmother's famous cookies and thought I'd bring them over."

"Thank you." Hudson took the cookies, feeling like they were a sugary bribe. He had no choice but to accept it, though, if he wanted him to leave quickly. "I appreciate you coming by. I've got to get back to work, though."

"I'll be on my way, but we need to get together and talk about my offer." He passed the cookies but didn't let them go. "Don't let Juniper discourage you from what you know is best for everyone. I know she can bat her eyelashes and make your good judgment get cloudy."

Hudson didn't like the way he spoke about Juniper. He straightened to match Ace's height. "I can assure you that no woman has ever dissuaded me from the appropriate business decision. I base my decisions on numbers and facts. And the fact is that there is a good reason for me to keep this property."

As if God was trying to teach him a lesson, a truck turned onto the main drive and barreled down on them.

"I think it's best you leave." Hudson thought about pushing the cookies back at the man, but Nana would scold him for being rude.

The truck slid to a stop, spitting rocks and dust

tainly they'd be home by dinner. If not, he could use the car he'd extended the rental on.

He opened his laptop and plopped down on the couch where he'd read to Gracie and tucked Juniper in for the night. His heart had been full then.

With a deep breath, he pushed his wayward thoughts away and studied the email the lawyer had sent. Not what he'd hoped but what he'd expected. His father could contest it if he wanted with his team of high-priced lawyers who always won their cases.

There was nothing he could do about that except hope his father didn't know about Nana's passing, so he searched through the documents his business associate had sent. After an hour of sifting through the zoning maps and property sales and identifying that they were all bought by shell companies, he saw it. His father's footprint. But why? The sales dated back over a decade. If it was his father, why didn't he ever develop the land?

None of it made sense.

Crunching gravel drew him to the window, but to his disappointment, it wasn't Juniper. It was Ace Gatlin. Great, what was he doing here again?

Hudson made his way outside hoping to get him to leave before Juniper came home and saw him here and made the assumption that Hudson was working behind her back.

into the air. Ace climbed into his own vehicle and revved the engine before Juniper could climb down.

"You best get off my land," she hollered at Ace, her eyes full of fire and passion and distraction. His distraction.

Juniper waited for Ace to drive away and then about-faced with a tight jaw and flailing arms. "You. I'm gone for a few hours and you're already conspiring to sell the land?" Juniper cried, tugging Hudson to her like she had an invisible string to his heart.

He opened the passenger door to find Gracie's face dotted with chocolate. "Someone enjoyed her ice cream today."

"Uh-huh, uh-huh." She swiped at her mouth with her tiny fists.

Before he could finish unbuckling and moving the straps out of the way, she had her arms out and wrapped around his neck. "Miss Hud."

He scooped the little girl up into his arms and hugged her tight, feeling the love filling that dark hole in his soul. Before he could ask her how the day went, Juniper tugged Gracie from him and marched into the house.

Hudson followed, hoping to speak to her and clear the air, but the second she had Gracie in her room, she returned with tight lines and quick steps.

"Wait. Let me explain. I told him no. I told him to get off the land." He spit the words out faster than a sour grape, but it didn't appear to douse her fire.

"You don't get it, do you?" Juniper took two steps into his personal space and put a finger to his chest. "You're going to stay long enough to take her home and her heart, then leave her more broken than when you found her."

Hudson touched Juniper's elbow. "Calm down. I don't understand."

Juniper shrugged him off her and paced the room. "Don't you see it? You always said you'd never hurt a child the way your father hurt you—that's why you could never be a father. But you got it wrong. It's not that you have a heavy hand, you have heavy words. Words that will devastate that little girl. Gracie deserves better than a man who will crush her. A man who will crush her with empty promises only to disappear the minute he gets what he wants."

The room tilted. Her words seared his heart and set his skin ablaze.

To harm a child. The one thing he promised he'd never do, and now she accused him of that. His chest tightened until he thought he couldn't breathe, but he did. He took one, two, three stuttered breaths and backed away. Away from the house, Juniper and, most of all, Gracie.

Chapter Eight

Juniper collapsed in the dining chair with her head in her hands. The wicker seat creaked, and the old wooden spindles moved under her weight the way her heart carried the weight of her words. Words that she knew had destroyed Hudson.

Comparing him to his father was a low hit. She regretted her words the minute they left her lips. Why did she have to go for the cruelest point instead of trying to speak with him?

She dropped her hands in her lap and looked at the ceiling. "I'm trying to open my heart, but You can't ask me to risk Gracie's."

Shame filled her with the realization she didn't have to be unkind with her words, but when she saw Ace in the driveway, she'd lost it. Hudson had said to trust him, and she hadn't. At the first sign of a test, she'd turned on him. But how could she trust him when her own husband had lied and stolen everything from her two seconds after he'd promised he'd never hurt her again?

She let out a failed-marriage breath. "I know Hudson isn't James, but I have to protect Gracie."

The sound of Gracie humming the *Little Einsteins* theme drew her from her thoughts to the living room, where she turned on the television for her daughter already sitting crisscross on the floor.

With Gracie engrossed in the show, she went to the window and eyed Hudson back at work. The man never rested. Maybe she'd misjudged him, and he had changed. She couldn't reconcile the man out there with the man who'd arrived a little over two weeks ago demanding she leave. She needed to protect Gracie. It was her biggest job as a mother, and she'd already failed her once.

As if Nana whispered in Juniper's ear, words fluttered into her mind: *Trust the Lord with all thine heart; And lean not into thine own understanding.*

With a sigh, and a glance over her shoulder to check on Gracie, she decided she needed to speak with Hudson to apologize and explain. She ventured outside and approached him as he pulled abandoned equipment from the shed.

For a moment, she stood there and watched him work, unsure of how to start the conversation. His muscles strained against the seams of his shirt and sweat poured from his temple. She glanced at the sky, but she knew this was on her to follow God's word and not her own mind. With a deep inhale of grass and flowers and sweat, she cleared her throat, but Hudson didn't turn around.

"I'm sorry," she said in the sincerest tone. "I should've trusted you when I saw Ace here. I'm apparently working on my trust issues. I know you believe in good business but—"

"I told him we'd never sell to him." He turned an old lawn mower over and examined the rusted blades. "He crossed a line. Apparently, business isn't the only thing I care about."

"Gracie?" Her gut clenched tight.

"Let's just say that over the course of a few conversations with the man, I've gleaned he's not a man I care to continue speaking with on this matter. Not when he disrespected you and Gracie, and if there's one thing I won't tolerate, it's disrespect, especially when he puts people down to get what he wants. He would've never said such things to Nana's face."

"No, he wouldn't. Nana had a way of putting the fear of God in everyone yet making you feel special all at the same time."

"She had a gift." Hudson took a wrench and hit the blade, sending rust raining down onto the lawn. "I won't break my promise, but I think we should speed things up," he said with a hint of worry in his tone.

"I went to town and filled out the business license application and zoning permit information for the hippotherapy." Juniper studied a ladybug crawling up the back of Hudson's shirt.

He dropped the wrench and sat back on his heels but didn't say anything.

"Listen, I was upset. I didn't mean to make you think you had to stay away from Gracie altogether. I just need you to keep some distance, and we need to make sure she understands you're not her father and you won't be staying."

"No, you were right, I shouldn't be around Gracie." His voice sounded distant, wounded.

"It's not because you're anything like your father. It's because I've already failed Gracie and I can't do it again. I'll never allow personal feelings to cloud my judgment when it comes to doing what's best for her."

He stood and wiped his hands on a rag. His eyes looked soft and sorrowful. She'd caused him to look like that. She hadn't been fair, but what was fair when a mother wanted to protect her child from more pain in her life? But the look made her want to pull him in for a hug, so she took a step back.

"You haven't failed Gracie. You've done everything you can for your daughter. You're not the one to blame for what's gone on in her life."

"I'm not some innocent little girl. I've made mistakes and all I can do is learn from them."

She eyed the house and knew she needed to get back before Gracie's TV show ended. "Listen, I'm sorry, but I didn't mean to run you off. I only want to protect my daughter from another person leaving her since it could cause irrevocable damage at this point. I can't risk it."

"Understood. All the more reason to work quick and get this done. I'll clean up, and after Gracie goes to bed, I'll come over. We need to sort out some final details so we can get this work done. After that, we need to make some decisions."

"There isn't an immediate rush. You can still be friendly with Gracie, just not eat all the meals at the table with her and take her for ice cream and have her hang out with you."

"We need to get this worked out because the lawyer says my father can contest the will and with his team of lawyers he has a shot at winning. My father once said that the minute Nana passed, he'd mow down the house that had trapped him inside all those years. He tried to put her in a condo years ago, but she wouldn't have it."

Juniper gasped and shook her head. "He doesn't have the right. Nana left the place to us."

"Maybe so, but you know my father." Hudson put his hands on his hips and eyed the farmhouse. "He almost convinced the county to push Nana out once, and if she hadn't put the fear of

God into the county commissioners, it might have happened." He snickered and shook his head. "I'd forgotten about that. It's part of the reason I left the second I got my college acceptance. I made a deal with the old man that I wouldn't be sucked into the farm life, and he would back off Nana's home."

The world went silent as if her ears had clogged to any other sounds long enough for her to process Hudson's words. The words she'd longed to hear for so long. A reason for him running away. She swallowed and closed her eyes for a second, but dizziness took hold, and she opened them to focus on a spot where the tree line met the road. The road Hudson had once taken out of her life.

And she finally knew why.

Hudson sat at the desk and eyed his nana's Bible while Juniper put Gracie in bed for the third time. The little one wanted him to read her a bedtime story, but Juniper wouldn't allow it. And he couldn't blame her. She was right. He'd be gone and it would harm Gracie even more than when he'd walked out on Juniper all those years ago.

He thumbed the gold-etched ends of the pages to feel closer to Nana. The smell of old paper and her perfume made him think that if he closed his eyes, he could imagine her standing by his side. If only she were here, she'd tell him what to do even if he didn't want to hear it. She always shared the best advice, not that he always listened.

The letter she'd left him—the one he'd read three times now—still didn't offer any clues about what she meant by more than he remembered. He racked his brain about his father and him. Did something happen between them that Hudson had blocked from his memories?

"Why is your father so determined to tear down this house? And does he still want to?" Juniper's soft voice drew him like the North Star breaking through the clouds.

He eyed the barn and the corral and the front pasture, and peace covered him in a way he never felt in the city. This farm had always been his place of respite growing up. "Because he blames this farm for getting my mother pregnant, forcing him to marry her and wasting so many years here doing the right thing."

"Ouch. Nana had told me he grew to resent your mother, and of course, I didn't understand it then, but I saw the bitterness on the few occasions he showed up here to get you after you'd run off."

Darkness floated in around him at the memories. "When I lost my mother, that big old house had nothing left in it but furniture and bad memories. She'd been the only light despite my father always saying she was worthless and an anchor against his sails. Whatever that meant."

"How often do you speak to him?" Juniper's hand touched his shoulder, chasing the bitterness away. He savored the contact, the comfort, the connection.

"Holidays and birthdays, his secretary sends a card, and on occasion when he's sealing a big deal he calls to try to pressure me into giving up that little resort business to come be his partner in the Kenmore empire."

Juniper squeezed as if to wring out the discomfort those words gave him. "You're a good man, Hudson Kenmore, and you don't need your father's approval any longer. According to Nana, he snapped after you were born, and he had to work at the feedstore to afford formula. He'd been valedictorian and accepted to an Ivy League school on scholarship, but he had no choice but to stay and marry your mother in those days. Nana said it was her biggest regret, telling her son he had to marry a woman and stay on the farm."

"I guess we all have our baggage, but he just needs to let it go."

Juniper backed away, taking her comfort with her, but he couldn't let it go, so he snagged her hand and held it to his cheek. "I'm sorry. You know I did everything I could to not make his mistakes."

"I know that now, but in the process of trying to impress him while avoiding hurting anyone the way he did, you lived a life of avoidance instead of acceptance. You've done well for yourself, there's no denying that, but has it made you happy?"

He faced her, holding her hand between both of his. "Are you happy?" His heart beat to a rhythmic tune, Juniper's tune. The only woman who'd ever made his pulse race and his chest fill with love and hope.

"I'm working through some things, but yes, I do have happiness in my life. I miss Nana and my father, but I have Gracie and God. I don't really remember much about my mother except my father telling me she was an honest, hardworking and stunning woman." Juniper closed her eyes for a second, opened them and looked at Hudson with such intensity. "What do you have, Hudson?"

He studied her chipped, unpolished nails, but her long, slender fingers didn't need all that paint. She had natural beauty, not to mention the glow she projected when she walked into the room. Funny how the women he'd attended business functions with glistened and glittered all over the place but had no glow. "How do you do it?"

"Do what?"

"Believe in happiness after all you've been through?" Hudson ran a thumb over her knuckles and his body felt lighter, like it would fly to

Heaven. Based on her parted lips and gaze transfixed on his thumb, she felt it, too.

"God. With God, there is always hope." She studied his hand, then swallowed loud enough for him to hear, and he saw it in her eyes—a determination to make life better. And more than anything, he wanted to do that for her, but she slid her hand free and walked away.

"I'll make us some hot cocoa and we can figure things out. If your father could potentially swoop in and claim this place, we both know he has the lawyers to do so. Because of that, you and I need to reach an agreement. A united front is our only hope."

Coldness settled over Hudson's skin. Perhaps from Juniper's exit or his worry over this farm turning into something beyond the respite it had always provided him. He placed his palm on the Bible and longed to feel the comfort and calmness that Juniper experienced through her nightly reading and daily prayer. Would God even want to hear from a man who'd turned his back on the Word to make a life for himself?

He closed his eyes and willed himself to pray, to welcome God back into his heart, but he didn't feel anything, nothing but the dead lump of nothingness in his chest. No, he'd created this life, and it was a good one. Happiness overflowed from Gracie into Juniper, as many kids did for their parents, but he'd done the right thing not bringing children into this world. He didn't possess the selfless love needed to have a family.

He shoved the Bible away and stood with his laptop in hand, then settled on the couch with the graphics, spreadsheets and zoning blueprints. The sound of cups clanking told him it wouldn't be long, but his anxiety simmered.

She returned, holding two mugs straight from his childhood. His mouth tugged into a smile despite his determination to remain serious and focused on business.

"I thought you could use the first aid mug. And Nana's promise of a smile is still guaranteed. I haven't seen that since you arrived."

He eyed the red-and-white mug that looked like Christmas in a cup, and he could almost taste the peppermint hot cocoa from the aroma alone. "She really did have a way of bringing joy and chasing off sadness. I miss her." He felt tears slip down his face. He swiped them away before they could reach his chin and averted his gaze.

Juniper set the mugs down on the side table and took his face in her hands. She lowered onto the couch next to him. "It's okay to feel it. It's okay to grieve. Have you shed any tears over her death?"

He sniffled and thought about pulling away, but the warmth she brought to the coldness in his bones hooked him and wouldn't let him go. She didn't stop there; she pulled him into her arms and held him tight. "It's okay to feel something. You don't always have to be perfect."

His throat closed and he felt the tears rushing in like a tsunami about to wash him away. He held her tightly like she'd be his link to salvation if he could keep hold of her long enough, but he couldn't. He couldn't have her believe in him. Not then, not now, not ever. He'd already hurt her once, and he knew he had no right to use her comfort for his pain, so he pulled away and bolted up. "You know real men don't cry."

He grabbed the mug and hid behind the rim so she couldn't see the tears in his eyes or his lip trembling. No way he'd ever let someone see him that weak.

"That's your father talking. A man who lost the woman who was a mother to him…he has a right to cry. I fear if he doesn't ever let his feelings in again, he'll be lost forever."

He took a sip of peppermint chocolate and savored the sweetness on his tongue. It took him a few seconds, but he managed to collect himself and face her. "There's nothing lost if he never existed."

Juniper shook her head and eyed her mug. "If only you could open your heart and realize you deserve happiness, then life could be better for us all."

The living room became small, too small. Juniper, sitting on the couch with her shiny hair draped over one shoulder, her bright eyes looking up at him with hope, was too much. He needed to escape this feeling of need. Need to have someone in his life that meant more than a passing thought. Juniper had always owned his heart, but he knew giving it to her would destroy them both, so he did the only thing he knew. He ran.

Chapter Nine

Juniper decided to remain inside with Gracie Monday morning to keep them separate despite her pleas to go help outside or to make Hudcakes. It had been days of working apart and keeping distance, and for a child, that was too long.

For Juniper, it had been too long.

With Gracie deep into her iPad with her thirty-minute timer by her side, Juniper stared at Hudson working outside. He never stopped. And he would never talk about his loss or pain.

She'd seen it in his eyes the other night, the agony he kept locked away. No person could carry that alone forever; someday he'd break, and she only hoped he'd have God in his life to help him put the pieces back together.

She averted her gaze to the computer at her desk and decided she'd been distracted for too long and needed to focus on writing out her business plan in which she focused on the benefits to the community instead of the revenue to the farm.

While waiting for the old computer to boot up,

she couldn't help but watch Hudson working at the shed. Later today, he'd move inside the house to work on renovations, so she'd have to allow Gracie to see him again.

The man out there worked off his grief with his hands. She could see that the more he worked, the more he was avoiding his feelings. If only he'd face things. But for a boy who knew nothing more about love than to avoid it, he'd never find true happiness, and she couldn't waste any time waiting on him to figure it out.

The screen lit up the room, so she opened her email and skimmed through the dozen or so advertisements but stopped on an official-looking Willow Oaks email with the title Violation of Residential Zoning Laws.

Her mouth went death dry. She clicked on the title and read through the long, attorney-style email about how her business license wasn't approved because of an outstanding fine for a violation but never specified what the violation was.

It had to be a mistake. Juniper glanced at Gracie and knew she had about ten minutes left before it was time to clean her room and get dressed, so Juniper snagged her cell phone and stepped out to the front porch where she'd have better reception.

She dialed the county offices and looked out over the green grass, watching a dragonfly flutter near the bushes Hudson had planted around the perimeter of the house.

The phone rang three times before the line cut in. "Planning and Zoning, Betsy here, how can I direct your call?"

"I received an email that my business license wasn't approved."

"Second, I'll transfer you."

The phone clicked and beeped. "County Business Services."

"Yes, I received an email that my business license wasn't approved because of a residential zoning issue."

"You'd need to speak to Residential Zoning about that, just a second, I'll transfer you."

The phone clicked and beeped again. Irritation pricked at Juniper. "Planning and Zoning, how may I direct your call?"

"Yes, I spoke to you, but you transferred me to the business office, and they transferred me back to you."

"If this is a business issue—"

"No, I received a violation notice."

"Oh, you'll need to speak with our appeals department."

Clicks and beeps.

"Appeals, how may I help you?"

Juniper took a breath. "Please, let me explain before you transfer me again. I received an email from the county stating my business license wasn't approved."

"That's—"

"That's not all. It was rejected because of a residential zoning violation."

"That's Planning and Zoning," she said in short, clipped words, obviously wanting to pass Juniper on to the next person.

"They transferred me here." Juniper rubbed her aching temple and noticed that the sound of hammering had stopped, so she searched the shed, but there was no sign of Hudson.

"I see. Well, you can appeal the violation. What is the violation for?"

"I don't know. There isn't an explanation."

"What is your name?"

"Juniper Keller."

"Second, I'll look you up."

Music came on telling Juniper this could be another minute, so she peered in through the window to see Gracie still mesmerized with her tablet. The dragonfly swooped from the roofline down to the porch and settled on the back of a rocking chair, its wings still fluttering as if he'd only rest a second. He had to be on a Hudson schedule.

The phone clicked. "No notice for a Juniper Keller."

"But I received an email."

"I'll transfer you back to the business office."

"But I already spoke to them." The phone clicked and beeped, tapping away at Juniper's temper.

"What's going on?" Hudson appeared around the side of the house, dirt covering him from head to toe, and he'd never looked so attractive. Something about a man who worked hard had always made Juniper's heart trot, but Hudson working hard took her imagination and ran a marathon.

He looked like he belonged there in his torn and rugged clothes more than any stuffy old suit.

She heard music, then more clicks, then more music, and finally she decided she was getting nowhere, so she hung up and huffed. "I've been slapped with a fine. I'm going into town to work it out."

The front door creaked open, calling Juniper's attention. Before she had time to process, Gracie raced past her, shimmied between the railing and flew off the porch into Hudson's arms.

Hudson chuckled. "Whoa there, you shouldn't jump without warning someone."

She giggled and threw her head back waiting to be spun, and Hudson obliged.

The sight was enough to make Juniper get lost for a moment in possibilities, but they weren't real, so she cleared her throat. "Gracie, we need to get ready and head into town."

"Stay Hud."

Hudson looked to Juniper, and for a second, she thought he was going to offer to watch Gracie for her, which tugged her in two different directions. She could use the time to focus on the business license, but then leaving her with Hudson to bond more would be a huge mistake.

"I'll be working on dangerous stuff, so you need to go with your mom today."

She slumped and cried out in his arms. "Hey, but I have a job that I need help with, do you think you can help me? I can't do it without you," he said.

Her little head flew up and she swiped her hair out of her face. "Uh-huh, uh-huh. I do."

He walked around holding her up in the air to fly until he reached the front steps and set her down. Then he pulled a screw from his pocket. "I need you to find one of these. It has to be exactly the same. The same length." He showed how long her finger was to the screw. "The width." He turned her finger to the side. "And how many twirls there are." He counted them off, then wrapped the screw in a bandanna and handed it to Gracie as if it were the secret to life.

Her mouth formed an O and she gasped.

"You do this for me?"

"Ye, ye." She saluted and clicked her heels together like a good soldier. She hadn't done that since Nana was alive.

How could a man who could hurt her also bring her out of her grief? Danger-ahead warnings blared in Juniper's head.

"You can't run with this. You have to walk with it pointed down. It's dull on the end, and the one you get will be sharp, so let your mom bring it home and you can give it to me. Deal?"

"Uh-huh, uh-huh." She turned with a spin too fast and almost fell over, but then heel-toe-walked inside with tiny steps at a slow pace.

"You shouldn't have done that," Juniper shot at him.

"I didn't call her over or come inside or break any of your other rules to keep us apart. I can't help it if she wants to be with me. Do you want me to be rude or mean?"

"No, but do you realize you just told yourself that you weren't your father? Too bad you won't listen to your own words." She about-faced and raced into the house like she was going AWOL from the Hudson boot camp of romantic thoughts.

To her surprise, she found Gracie dressed and ready before Juniper even finished brushing her teeth. Without one complaint, Gracie climbed into the truck, holding that screw inside the bandanna and studying it like it had all the answers to all her questions. She didn't even complain when they waited in line at the county offices and were sent to three different departments only to discover no one knew anything and her only choice was to leave a message for the employee who did the filing and hadn't passed it up the chain of command, who would be out for two days. Gracie didn't even cry out at the flickering light in the one room, so Juniper couldn't complain when Gracie wanted to study every screw in the hardware store to make sure she got the exact duplicate for Hudson.

The man had been brilliant. He could deny it all he wanted, but Hudson was born to be a father. It was the husband part he wouldn't do well at.

They returned home and Juniper felt defeated, so defeated she allowed Gracie to take the screw to Hudson and for him to walk her back to the house while she snagged the Bible and sat on the couch holding it to her chest with her eyes closed, hoping to overcome her headache.

She must've dozed off, because the next thing she knew Gracie was patting her face. "Momma, Momma. Hud, din."

The aroma of hearty meat and potatoes with a hint of paprika told her Hudson had made Nana's famous fried chicken. Her stomach growled and she shot up, the Bible falling to the floor with a thump.

Hudson arrived with the ruffled-sleeved apron

and picked up the Bible. "I know I shouldn't be here, but you were asleep, and Gracie was hungry."

She couldn't scold him; he'd taken care of Gracie and allowed her to rest. "No, I mean thank you. I had a headache and thought I'd close my eyes for a minute. I'm glad you're here."

Gracie ran into the kitchen, squealing and full of life.

Juniper pointed to where her daughter just flew by. "That's the problem, though. I can't rely on you because you'll be gone soon, and Gracie and I will be alone again."

"I understand." Hudson offered his hand to help her stand.

"I feel bad for the way I reacted. It's just that it's difficult to protect Gracie and be nice to you. I don't know why." She chuckled. "I'm sorry. I mean you even made dinner for us."

"Don't feel bad. It wasn't an entirely selfless act. I wanted to come inside to search for the box you mentioned." His jaw twitched.

"Did you find it?" Juniper asked, forcing herself to concentrate on putting one foot in front of the other with Hudson so close to her.

"No, I'm afraid not. I hope to search some more soon. It's bothering me that there's something I apparently don't remember. It's like a puzzle I can't solve." Hudson pulled out her chair and they all sat down around the big circle table in the kitchen.

In that moment she wanted him to stay, to be Gracie's father, to be her husband, to be their everything.

She closed her eyes and prayed, "Lord give me strength."

Hudson sat at the table watching the girls enjoy the dinner he'd made for them, thankful Nana insisted he learn to cook. Not that he'd used his skills in years.

Gracie picked up a leg and bit into it. "Ummm. Ummmmmmm." Her eyes opened wide, and she dropped the leg onto the plate with chicken sticking out of her mouth.

Juniper didn't notice since she dug into her own meat.

Satisfaction didn't begin to describe how he felt watching them. How many meals did he eat at five-star restaurants making huge deals and walking away with a sense of accomplishment? Never had he ever felt this much joy during a meal, though.

Gracie picked up her special fork and pierced a string bean and giggled. "I do. I do."

"Yes, you do," Hudson reassured her, patting her on her tiny back. Who knew such a little thing could shine so bright.

Juniper paused and set her drumstick down, then wiped Gracie's face with her napkin. "I forgot how good Nana's chicken was. Thank you for this."

Tears filled her eyes, and he knew it was more tears of joy than sadness. She was right about one thing: he hadn't fully processed his loss, but his father had a point, too. No time for crying over things when you could do something about it. And he was—he was going to help Juniper and Gracie. He only hoped his paranoia about his father was unfounded. Still, that nervous itch in the back of his neck remained.

"Thanks to Nana for insisting boys should know how to cook as well as run a tractor." He took a bite off his own chicken and enjoyed the crunch of the outside with the juicy inside. The pepper and paprika set off a memory explosion. "Do you remember the last time we ate this together?"

A blush dusted Juniper's cheek. She glanced at him, then averted her gaze. "Yes, of course I do. I'm just surprised that you do."

He choked down a few green beans past the lump that kept rising in his throat each time he dipped his memory into the past. "Never forgot that day." And he hadn't because it was the day of their epic kiss.

Gracie finished her plate and hopped down to

set it on the counter. A few seconds later, the *Little Einsteins* theme song sounded from the other room. Hudson knew the routine—half hour of television, book reading, bed.

Juniper stood and cleared the dishes. "You cook, I clean."

"Dishwasher hasn't been fixed yet, so I'll dry." He took his place at the sink by her side and couldn't take his eyes off her. Who knew that a woman could look so beautiful washing dishes?

"Why are you staring at me?"

He couldn't help but reach up and tuck the hair behind her ear to see her better, finding her cheek as soft as he remembered. "I can't help it. You're still the most beautiful woman I've ever known."

Instead of a smile, she stiffened at his side. "Please, I've seen the pictures of the great Hudson Kenmore's beautiful and broken women. I think they line four New York City blocks."

He stepped back. "I'm sorry. I didn't mean to make you uncomfortable."

"It's not that." Juniper rinsed a bowl, handed it to him and then sighed.

"Then what is it?"

"You tell me these things. You've never lacked the ability to give a good compliment, but there's no meaning behind it. They're only empty words all about physical appearance that you sprinkle around to make yourself feel better."

"Make myself feel better? How does giving you a compliment make me feel better? If anything, it hurts."

"Me or you?" She challenged him, the way she'd always challenged him. It was one thing he loved…no, liked about her. The one woman who made him a better man.

He dried the plate and set it aside. "I don't mean to hurt you. I only want you to know how truly special you are and how you deserve the absolute best in life."

"I have the best in life." She handed him another plate and this time she looked at him with her soft eyes and hopeful expression. "Even if you don't think life is worth anything without money."

"I agree, the old adage that money can't buy happiness is true. Yet, without money, life is more difficult." Hudson set the plate down and faced her and the truth. "What would've happened if we got married out of high school and we had a child we couldn't afford? If I couldn't put food on the table or buy formula for our child? I could've never faced a life like that, watching you suffer, and we both knew we'd grow to resent each other."

"We didn't know that."

"Didn't we? We had proof. My parents. My mother died lonely of a broken heart."

"Your mother had a genetic heart condition," she countered, her voice raised. She leaned back to see the living room, and he knew she was checking on Gracie. "You need to trust the Lord will provide."

"Where was God when my mother died?" he choked out. Tears welled up, but he swallowed them down. "Listen, I'll call my lawyer tomorrow and he'll dig into why there's a violation. Then—"

"No."

He blinked at Juniper as if to see her words more clearly. "What? Why?"

"I'll be dealing with the county. You want to invest in supplies to fix up the place, that's fine. I believe Nana wanted us both to have a place here, so I have no desire to take over." She drained the sink.

"And you don't want me to take over either."

"No. I'm fine with that if it protects this place, but like I've been trying to tell you, there's more to happiness besides money. I came here after the divorce to give Gracie a chance at having a home. A real home. A respite from the world."

Hudson looked at the old linoleum floor where the seam split across the kitchen the way his heart split in two. "A respite?" Hadn't this place been exactly that for him? How could he deny Gracie a place to feel safe and loved from a world that frightened her? How could he give any less than his nana had given him? "I'll do it."

"What?" Juniper studied him as if to read the lines around his eyes for clues to his meaning.

"I'll help get the hippotherapy program up and running."

Juniper nodded and held out her hand. "I'll deal with the business stuff, and you can continue to work on the house renovations."

"Wait, I'm the businessman here."

"And I'm the one with the plans, the grant research and the heart to make this work." She took a step into his space. "Thank you, but I'm in charge of the program. You can do whatever you want with the other land, but I'll show you I can make this work on my own." She stood up on her toes and pressed her lips to his cheek and he thought he'd lost all sense. That simple kiss caused complicated thoughts. He wanted to tell her he'd stay and run a hippotherapy program on the farm and give up all his financial security to stay with her.

Chapter Ten

Juniper dropped the official county document on the table. "I can't believe it's taken four days to find out the code violations. This is ridiculous." Her skin heated but she said a silent prayer to tame the anger welling up inside.

"Hud. Hud. Brush?"

Hudson took the brush from Gracie and sat on the floor.

Juniper glanced over her shoulder, waiting to see him tending to a little girl's hairstyle. This would be interesting.

She worked on a list of the ridiculous items from the letter.

"It's a game to keep you from succeeding."

A pinch of worry broke through her resolve to remain calm. "Your father?" Her gaze lingered on him for a few extra seconds, admiring the sight of him tenderly brushing Gracie's thin blond hair.

"I thought I was being paranoid, but maybe. But my father isn't usually this subtle. Trust me.

He's more of the bulldozer-and-lawyers type. This is sneakier and doesn't show much power."

"Not much power? Whoever did this stopped my business license from going through."

"Only delayed. We'll reapply once we do those things and pay the fine."

Juniper saw the wisps of hair falling from the too-loose, not-so-braided braid, so she went to lend a hand.

"No. Hud do."

"If you want Hudson to do this then I need to show him how. He doesn't know how to deal with little wiggling girls like you." Juniper poked her in the side and made her squirm and giggle.

Juniper wanted to tell Gracie again how Hudson wouldn't be staying, but no matter how many times she explained it to her last night and this morning, Gracie decided to hear what she wanted. It would be impossible to keep them apart at this point with all the work and needing to trust the only person in the world she could to help keep an eye on her daughter while they did renovations and paperwork.

Like it or not, they'd be a team for as long as it took to fix up this place. She took Hudson's hands in hers, ignoring the spark of energy shooting up from her fingers, and guided him to weave Gracie's hair into a tight braid until he got the rhythm.

She retreated from the comfort and excitement she hadn't felt since she was a teenager. "I almost forgot, I think I found the box that I told you Nana had mentioned when I was cleaning out the hall closet. It might be what she was talking about because it's labeled *Hudson*."

He rose and followed her gesture to the hallway where he knelt. "What's inside?"

"Don't know. Your name was on it, so I didn't open it."

Gracie ran to the box. "I open. I open."

Hudson sat back while she tugged until the box lid snapped free. Juniper joined them, looking over their shoulders. "What's inside?"

He lifted out a picture of him and his mother and father when he was a baby. "They almost look happy there." His voice sounded distant and wanting.

"They do. See, there were some good times," Juniper offered.

"Maybe." He shrugged, set the picture aside and then Gracie handed him baby shoes. "Looks like stuff from when I was little."

Another photo of him and his parents without a frame and this one was torn in half. Only his parents' faces and the top of his head showed. The box also held a rattle and a pink baby dress with little blue flowers embroidered on it.

"What's that?" He held it up for Juniper to tell him.

She eyed it and shook her head. "Not one of Gracie's. I don't know."

A few other girl things rested in the bottom—a baby brush, a jacket and little pink booties. "Strange."

Gracie sighed and dropped her hands in her lap, then shot up and ran for the door. Apparently, nothing in the box interested her.

Hudson shoved the box under the hallway table and brushed his legs free of dust as he stood, disappointment etched on his face. "Time to get to work."

"I help." Gracie grabbed her pink faux toolbox and marched out the front door with her head held high.

Hudson scooted up by Juniper before she realized he'd moved. "Her speech is improving. More words, and did you notice? The light flickering in the hall didn't set her off," he whispered in her ear before moving on and leaving her behind in the house.

He'd noticed? The man smiled back at her with pride in his eyes that squeezed Juniper's heart. "It's good. I just hope she doesn't struggle when you leave." She didn't want to get in an argument, and the twitch of his cheek warned her to change the subject. "What do you think those little baby girl things were about?" she asked.

"Don't know. It's a mystery to me. Probably something left over from years ago. Maybe it's Nana's and she's trying to send me a message to settle down and have babies. I wouldn't put it past her."

Juniper chuckled. "Neither would I." She assumed it was Nana's way of showing him that Gracie could be his daughter, but he chose to ignore her message. But Juniper wanted this. A partner in life to watch Gracie grow up, to applaud her accomplishments, doctor her hurts and hug her tears away. But that man wasn't Hudson, and she wasn't some little girl who'd blindly love a guy again. This was all she wanted, the farm to raise Gracie where she'd benefit from home-based therapy. And she didn't need a man to do that. She'd been doing okay on her own. Not that it would be easy with hiring therapists and running the business side of things, but she'd manage.

Nana had been right about many things, but Hudson and Juniper ending up together was her one mistake.

With list in hand and a duffel of toys, Juniper followed Hudson to the fence line at the edge of the property. Things were looking better. The barn repairs were complete, chicken coop fixed, landscaping done and fields mowed. She didn't like having to leave the safety of the barn, corral and home, though, since she knew keeping an eye on Gracie without an alarm could be challenging. And Gracie couldn't help with the wire since she could get cut, so Juniper hoped her favorite toys would keep her busy. She spread a blanket on the ground. "Sit here, hon. The grass won't itch through this blanket. And here's your puzzle and iPad."

Gracie folded her arms over her chest. "No, I help."

Juniper looked at the golden toy of hours of distraction. The iPad always worked. "But I'll let you play on your iPad for more than thirty minutes."

Gracie stuck her lip out, dropped her hands to her side and grumbled in a defeated tone. "I help."

"If you think you're big enough, I could use a special helper," Hudson said.

Gracie's attention snapped to him, eyes wide with a teeth-showing smile. "I special help."

"She can't cut wire and string it. It's too dangerous."

He glanced over his shoulder with a raised brow before he looked back at Gracie. "I need these sorted." He retrieved a box from the bag and handed it to Gracie. "Do you know your colors?"

"Uh-huh, uh-huh."

"Okay, I need all the zip ties to go in the right slots. Black here, blue here, yellow here and red here." He pointed to the different spots in the tackle box. "Once you're done with that, come straight to me, because I have an even bigger job."

Juniper stood there in awe. Since when would her daughter ever deny iPad time? The man was brilliant. It was like he'd read the Gracie handbook no one ever gave Juniper. Gracie wouldn't budge until her job was done. There would be no interrupting her or changing until the task was complete. For the first time, she saw Gracie's lack of being able to transition and her obsession at completing a task as a gift instead of a challenge.

"You might want to close your mouth before you get a horsefly in there." Hudson grabbed the wire cutters and went to work removing the area with the broken and dangerous wires that could apparently cause bodily harm to people and roaming animals according to the county violation notice.

Juniper rolled out a section and helped Hudson move it into place to fasten it to the log posts. "Fence's been around for as long as I can remember."

"Yeah, from the stories my father told me, my grandfather and him put this fence in when he was a child. Says he had blood, sweat and tears on this wire."

The chicken wire protested, but she managed to keep it against the wood. "Needs replacing, but to do it right along the entire property line would call for a permit, and something tells me that if our good friend Ace is at the heart of this, he'd make sure to stall that permit. Not sure what he's up to, but he's determined to win this land one way or another."

"I agree. Still not sure if it's my father or Ace but doesn't matter. We can always replace the fence later."

They worked until the section was complete, then moved to the next area and the next and then the next. For hours they worked and relocated, and each time they moved, Hudson waited for Gracie to finish the project she worked on and had another one ready to go at the next spot. He kept her in the shade, placing the blanket down after checking for anthills and any kind of danger, and returned to work.

Juniper could barely stand up by the end of the day, but she needed to make sure she put a good meal on the table for Hudson after he'd cooked for her and worked all day and taken care of Gracie. By the time they were done eating, Gracie fell asleep before her episode of *Little Einsteins* even finished. Hudson lifted her into his arms and carried her to bed before Juniper could even get off the couch.

She snagged Gracie's favorite bear left behind on the floor and went to her room to find the most beautiful sight she'd ever seen. Hudson tucked the covers under Gracie's chin, brushed the hair from her eyes and kissed her forehead. "Night night, little squirrel."

Call it exhaustion or emotions, she wasn't sure, but the room tilted so she leaned against the doorjamb to stay upright. Her heart beat fast and hard.

When Hudson stood up and faced Juniper, she saw the truth. She'd not only failed to protect Gracie from getting her heart broken, but her own would be smashed and scattered like ashes when he left her…again.

Each day for the past two weeks, Hudson had gotten up early to have breakfast, work for several hours on renovations, have lunch, check email, work on renos, have dinner, play with Gracie, read stories, check email and go to bed. But this morning, Hudson found himself waking up and not thinking about any work beyond the farm. Strange, considering he'd been gone from corporate for two weeks longer than he'd planned and didn't even worry about some hostile takeover or loss of money. But he did worry for Mark since he hadn't returned Hudson's last two messages.

Little Gracie waited at the edge of the top step with her toes hanging over, obeying the rule not to go beyond the porch to find him. An issue they'd discovered the second morning, when he'd woken up with Gracie standing at the bottom of the stairs holding his morning coffee. He couldn't be mad, but shock didn't describe what he felt opening his eyes to a little girl staring down at him.

Since that day, the alarm stayed on until he came and knocked on the front door or when Juniper brought him his coffee outside.

He hurried up and messed her hair before taking the cup. "Thanks, hon." Since when had he ever been so eager to get out of bed in the morning?

"Uh-huh. Uh-huh." She giggled and ran back inside. "I give. I give."

Juniper stood at the stove whipping up some eggs, the aroma filling the room with the promise of a hearty breakfast before work. Routine, that was what they'd fallen into. Despite how close Gracie had gotten to him, Juniper had grown that much more distant.

She wasn't the follower any longer. She'd led him around pointing out jobs, filling out paperwork, all while taking care of Gracie. Juniper had grown from the young girl he'd known into an independent and determined woman like no other he'd ever met. But she remained at arm's length at all times.

He spotted the Bible on the table and knew she'd already done her morning devotion. Her faith was unshakable, and he envied that. Another sin to add to his "bad Christian" list. "What was the passage this morning?"

"What?" Juniper slid two fried eggs on top of some toast and put it on the table in front of him.

"The verse that you read this morning?"

"Unfortunately, I overslept, so I didn't get a chance yet. If you don't mind, I'll be a couple of minutes late getting out to the field today."

"Hud read?" Gracie crawled up into the chair and scooted the Bible next to his plate.

"No need to bother Hudson, we'll read after breakfast." Juniper grasped the Bible, but something came over him and he gently pried it from her fingers. He wanted to open Nana's Bible and hear something, anything, to help him understand why he'd found happiness in the one place he'd avoided for so long. Wisdom on how to reconcile the life he'd created and the one he'd fallen into and how to reconnect with God the way Juniper did. He wanted that kind of strength.

"No worries. Do you know what passage you were going to read?"

She turned off the stove and slid the pan to the side. "No, I let God decide."

He scratched his chin. "Ah, how does that work?"

"I open the book and flick through until it stops, and I put my finger down on a passage. Not scientific, but it seems to always give me the words I need to hear."

She gave Gracie her plate and special fork, then retrieved her own food and sat next to him. "Seriously, I can do it after breakfast, or now if you prefer to listen."

"No, I've got this." He wanted to be a man worthy of sitting at Nana's table. A man worthy of Gracie. A man worthy of Juniper.

He swallowed a gulp of coffee to calm his nerves, took a breath and opened the Bible, allowing the pages to flip until they stopped.

Gracie hopped up on her knees and stuck her finger on a verse. "This one."

Hudson smiled at her enthusiasm and couldn't bear to disappoint her. "Okay, you ready?"

"Uh-huh. Uh-huh."

Juniper bit her bottom lip and nodded. Were those tears in her eyes? He couldn't look again in fear he'd lose his nerve to read from the Bible. A book and faith he'd left behind to find his own way in life.

What had that gotten him? A lot of money. That's what.

But was Juniper right and money wasn't where a person found joy?

Hudson cleared his throat. "1 Timothy 17-18: 'Charge them that are rich in this world, that they be not high-minded, nor trust in uncertain riches, but in the living God, who giveth us richly all things to enjoy; That they do good, that they be rich in good works, ready to distribute, willing to communicate.'"

His voice cracked. A powerful surge of truth battered down his walls of self-indulgence and self-protection. He dared a quick glance at Juniper, who had a knowing smile. She took his hand and Gracie took his other.

"Dear Lord, thank You for this food and for all the gifts You've brought into our lives. The roof over our heads, the food on our table and our health. We thank You for these gifts. In Jesus' name we pray, amen." She squeezed his hand. The simple gesture spoke volumes of how she saw the breakthrough he'd just made in his faith. Had he, though?

It was easy to hear words and feel something. A completely different situation to act on them. He dug into the salty goodness of the fried eggs and bacon while his mind reeled with possibilities of change.

Gracie sniffled and wiped her nose in between playing with her food, causing Juniper to send her to her time-out mat, but Hudson didn't say a word. He couldn't, not when all his thoughts had been taken and churned and captured in a pool of hope he didn't dare jump into. Not right now. Now he only needed to concentrate on the work ahead, so he cleared their plates and did the dishes while Juniper had Gracie in her room getting ready to head outside.

Hudson didn't wait, not this time, because he needed some air and some distance. Fresh air offered him a reprieve to drink another cup of coffee and look out over the land. The sun rose to the canopy where only a hint of the orange glow shot a bright light over the pasture and barn and life. A deer scurried from one side of the farm to the other with a fawn by her side.

"A bucket for your thoughts?"

He hadn't heard Juniper opening the front door, so the touch to his back took him by surprise a second after her words. The warmth of her hand so potent after two weeks of little physical contact. She'd kept two feet between them except when he'd read the Bible verse and she took his hand earlier. "Not anything you want to hear, I'm sure."

Juniper rubbed between his shoulder blades. "I know it can be difficult to open your heart again to God, but trust He knows the truth you can't see yourself."

He spun around and found himself close to Juniper, so close he thought she stole his breath. "It's that and so much more."

A bird swooped down and landed on the banister as if Nana sent the red cardinal to chastise him into spilling his darkest fears and brightest hopes to his June Bug. A woman who showed such strength he almost believed he wouldn't break her the way his father had broken his mother. "It's you. You and Gracie."

"What about us?" She slid back a step, but he snagged her pinky and she stopped.

His breath came in short bursts, but he needed to tell her how he felt in some way or form. "June Bug… Sorry. I forgot you don't like it when I call you that." He sighed.

"Don't mind. Kind of like it now that you're not behaving like you're committing corporate takeover of the farm."

He chuckled. "That bad?"

"Worse, but it's okay." She winked, and her smile that warmed him to the core made a brief appearance. "Tell me. You can trust me."

After one more deep breath, he managed to say, "You're not the person I knew when I left."

She eyed the splintered front porch. "Sorry if I disappoint you."

"No." He tipped her chin up to look at him. "You're more. The strength you have is something I've seen in no other woman I've ever known. You're an amazing mother to a special little girl who is growing up with such a spark in this gray world. You've turned her life into your mission, and you do it with such grace. How you've managed to stay true to your faith without question is indescribably beautiful."

"Thanks. I try, but I couldn't do it without my faith. No one can take on life's challenges and feel good without faith. Faith is what keeps me going when I think life is too hard."

Desire to touch her, to connect with her and God, drew his hand to her cheek. "You don't understand. I've never felt this passionate about my job, not like I do about this farm, about you and Gracie." *Say it.* A voice, his inner voice, whispered in his head. But he couldn't. How could he tell her he was falling in love with her when he didn't know how to face it himself?

Chapter Eleven

Hudson sat on his bed feeling restless despite his muscle-aching work. The sounds of crickets chirping and frogs croaking usually lulled him to sleep, but how could he sleep with the realization he had feelings for a woman he'd tossed aside to make his life what it was today?

No. He'd left for a reason. In his core, he knew he was just like his father. A man who only spoke to his son when he was trying to dissolve Hudson's company into Kenmore Enterprises or telling him what a mistake he was making for not wanting to be part of his father's legacy.

He eyed his phone and Nana's Bible on the desk. The Bible Juniper insisted he take back to his room tonight. Not sure why, but he didn't want to take time to argue about bringing the book with him when he was trying to escape so he could figure out how he truly felt about everything.

Instead of picking up the Bible, he grabbed his

laptop from his bag and managed to use the Wi-Fi booster he'd installed to pull down his mail.

His partner had emailed him that all was fine, and he was living his best life and promised he was already working on the next deal and included some details for Hudson's approval.

He felt relieved about Mark doing well and didn't even have a hint of his bulldog instinct to get involved with their next business venture.

Without even looking at most of the links, he typed, You decide. I trust you.

Before he shut down his laptop, he decided to pull up Juniper's business plan and the guidelines for starting a hippotherapy program. She'd been thorough, addressing the difference between equine therapy, which she'd already completed training and certification for, and hippotherapy, which she'd have to hire a therapist for.

Impressed, he found himself drawn to research the goals and achievements of all types of horse therapies. That spark that had been missing since the last deal rapid-fired as he went through evidence-based research about the benefits of the program. He'd never seen such joy in the faces of wounded vets, children with physical and mental disabilities, and all sorts of people with challenges.

Juniper truly had a heart for helping others, but did he? Just because he found himself excited about something didn't mean he was worthy to be involved. What if they failed? He'd never failed at any business in his life.

He'd only failed at relationships. All of them. He'd never opened his heart to anyone since he'd left, not even to his nana.

Conviction took hold and he eyed the Bible sitting on the desk like a clue waiting to be deciphered.

His email dinged and he glanced at the message from his partner.

Where is Hudson Kenmore and what have you done to him?

Hudson didn't want to leave him hanging, so he replied, I'm going to be staying a little longer than I thought, looking into a business op here. You move forward at corporate. I trust you.

He shut his laptop, ending the conversation, and set it aside to pick up the Bible. Heavy in his hand from the weight of the grief that still plagued him, but was he ready to open the book and his heart and mind to the possibility of bringing God back into his life?

They'd been distant friends at best after his mother's passing and complete strangers since he'd left the farm. Would He even want to hear from Hudson or had He given up on him years ago?

He spent an hour staring at the black book

with gold writing on the cover before he finally opened it the way Juniper said she and Nana did, letting the pages flip until they rested. He closed his eyes, remembering Gracie's tiny finger pointing at the page. He looked to find his finger on 2 Corinthians 2:10.

To whom ye forgive anything, I forgive also: for if I forgave anything, to whom I forgave it, for your sakes forgave I it in the person of Christ.

Hudson sank onto the bed, elbows on knees, book closed between his hands and head down. "Are You asking me to forgive my father? The man who caused my mother to die of a broken heart? To forgive him for telling me I was never good enough? For his heavy hand and heartless nature? Is that the only way I can be welcomed back into Your flock? It's too much. You ask too much."

The night grew darker as did his heart. He abandoned the Bible on the desk and ignored his phone. No way he'd contact his father. Not now. What if his father really didn't know about the farm and Hudson sparked his father's interest and he swooped in to ruin everything, every chance at a happiness he still didn't believe he deserved?

No. It wasn't right.

Hudson crawled into bed hugging his pillow and holding it tight to his chest, and tears flowed down his cheeks. Tears for the loss of his mother, loss of his nana, loss of Juniper, loss of God.

Sobs welled up years of pain and suffering until he thought he'd die of his own broken heart. Juniper had called him out for his distance and not allowing himself to feel anything. But this hurt. Feelings felt foreign and raw and vulnerable.

Images of holding his mother's hand while sitting on the floor by her side, hearing the sirens in the distance, watching her slip from this life. It shredded him until the sorrow ravaged him into complete silence, unable to scream or cry out as if he'd suppressed it for so long it couldn't escape.

Flashes of his father's cold words—*Now maybe you'll let go of foolish feelings and become a real man*—dislodged the cry and he let it out, howling like a wounded coyote.

Memories simmered of his visits to the farm, his escape from reality with his father. Happiness surged over him like a salve applied to a wound, and he welcomed the touch of hope. Nana's love had been the only light, but it hadn't been enough to weaken his hate for a man who'd caused him so much grief and a God who hadn't saved him.

He sniffled and coughed the last bits of hate and rolled over on his back to look out the small window at the stars twinkling in the dark sky. "Nana, I never told you how much you meant to me. I'm so sorry I wasn't here when you passed.

Even if I knew you were sick, I'm not sure I could've faced it. To hold your hand the way I'd held my mother's." The words choked him.

His eyes grew heavy, and he welcomed the escape, but even in sleep, he couldn't run anymore. Dreams of his future took hold, and he had no way to free himself from the truth that he had reached a choice—either continue on the safe path and return to his old life or choose the rocky road full of dangers that offered a greater reward.

Even when the first rays of light woke him, he didn't see the sunlight as a sign of what was yet to come. He'd made a turn but only found himself lost in the middle of nowhere, with no understandable directions.

Hudson entered the house with his head down and bent shoulders—not the confident, strong and put-together man Juniper had always known. Something had happened. She wouldn't push him to talk about it, but she feared that look meant he'd be leaving soon.

Gracie crawled up on his lap at the kitchen table and snuggled into him while he drank his morning coffee. His eyes appeared as if he'd been crying, but that wasn't possible. Hudson Kenmore might get choked up, but he never cried.

Perhaps he'd finally faced the loss of his nana.

Gracie sniffled and climbed down without her

usual bright smile and shuffled out of the kitchen without a word.

"Go brush your teeth so we can get to work." Juniper abandoned the last few breakfast dishes and settled into the chair by his side. The rich aroma of the strong farm coffee drew her to sip on her second cup.

"She okay?" He eyed Gracie shuffling down the hallway.

Juniper nodded. "She gets tired sometimes and when she does, she gets cranky and doesn't want to do her chores. I told her she couldn't take you coffee until she got her teeth brushed, so she's upset with me."

The tension showed in his tight cheeks…further evidence he struggled. "What's on your mind?"

The old pipes rattled, telling her Gracie worked on her teeth finally, giving them a minute, but he remained silent, studying his mug.

She couldn't take it anymore and covered his hand that clung to the mug handle. "What is it?"

"Do you think Nana knew that I cared about her and that I wanted to be here for her but…" His voice trailed off to some far-off place.

Juniper squeezed his hand. "Nana knew you loved her. She defended you to the end. I'd criticize you for not coming around, and she'd tell me how it had little to do with you wanting to stay away and more to do with you not being able to face your fears."

Hudson's head snapped to the side, his eyes wide. "She should've told me she was so ill. It should've been my choice."

Juniper hesitated, her heartbeat against her ribs slow and strong. "I didn't mean to upset you."

"No, tell me everything she said."

Juniper studied the crack running around the handle that she'd superglued back together when Gracie had dropped it trying to take coffee to Hudson the first day. "The older she got, the less she told you, because she never wanted you to have to witness another one you loved passing away. She said she'd seen it before. A man breaking in half when they have too many or too great of losses."

The pain etched in the lines around his eyes nipped at her resolve to tell him how much she'd resented his treatment of a woman who offered him so much. A woman he'd abandoned. But she saw something beyond her judgment. She saw the wound that had been festering for so long in his soul. The wound that had driven him away. "She was right. Until you learn to face your past, your heart will never heal. Until your heart heals, you'll never find a way to allow someone else into your life. You'll remain alone and lost."

"You think I'm alone? That I'm broken and

haven't had a decent life?" His gaze narrowed and his nose flared. "I've had an excellent life. I'm worth a lot of money. Not my father's level but plenty to stop working and live the rest of my life in style and comfort."

"I have no doubt." Juniper realized this wasn't a fight she wanted to take on because it wasn't hers to battle. "I've always known you'd be successful. You're intelligent, gifted, determined and talented."

"Yet you think I live an empty life." His words were bitter, but she saw his anger wasn't at her but at himself.

She took her coffee mug to the sink to wash it. "I didn't say that."

"You're right." His words sounded rough and shaky. "I've made a lot of mistakes in my life, but leaving here wasn't one of them, because I was too broken to be the man you deserved back then."

She froze. Her pulse tapped and thrashed at her neck. Air trapped in her lungs, but she had to turn around. A million questions flooded her mind, but she settled on the main one. *Is he ready now to be that man?* A man who would want to run the farm by her side, to help raise Gracie, to love her?

One, two, three breaths. She set the mug down in the sink, wiped her hands and turned to face him, but he was gone. Only his half-empty mug left on the table as evidence he'd even been there a moment before.

No, not this time. They needed to finish this conversation. She wouldn't let him walk out without telling her he was leaving. She marched out of the kitchen to give him a piece of her mind, but instead of finding him running away, she spotted him entering Gracie's room.

She went down the hall to find Hudson kneeling by Gracie's bed tucking the covers under her chin. "I'm so sorry you don't feel well, little squirrel." He retrieved her favorite bear on the floor and shimmied it down in the covers by her side.

"I sick." She sniffled and stuck out her lip.

He pressed his forehead to hers. "I think we should all take a rest today. Do you want Nana's special medicine?"

"Make better?"

"It helps with sniffles and fever and sore throats."

"I fever?" Gracie asked, placing the back of her hand to her forehead in her best Southern fainting pose.

"Think so. Is your throat ouchie?" Hudson touched a finger to her neck.

"Itchy."

Juniper had thought Gracie was just tired but

could she have strep again? Nothing an antibiotic wouldn't cure but she felt bad for not noticing sooner.

Hudson sat on the side of the bed. "Nana's special drink will help that, too. I'll make it for you. Do you like peppermint?"

"Uh-huh. Uh-huh." She sniffled again.

"I'll be back with that in a minute. You stay here and rest."

Gracie shot up and wrapped her arms around him. "Luv you."

Juniper froze, waiting for Hudson to pry her arms away and run faster than a wild mustang shot across a grassland.

"I love you, too, sweet girl."

Juniper backed from the room and leaned her head against the wall behind her. Had Hudson used the L-word? Sure, he'd been trapped in the arms of a little girl, but he could've run away. He was good at that.

So many emotions swirled and twirled around inside her. One thought screamed she should've kept to her vow to keep him away from her daughter. Another thought shouted for her to give him a chance to be a different man, but that could prove to be a dangerous game. A game that could cause her daughter to regress after so much progress. Progress she'd made because of the man she wanted to keep her from.

Hudson entered the hall, running a hand through his hair. His gaze darted about like a frightened frog. "Should I go get a doctor? Medicine? What can I do to help?"

"Calm down." Juniper smiled at his worried expression. "It's a cold or might be strep throat."

"Strep? You go start the truck. I'll carry her out."

She placed a hand on his chest and felt his heart pounding like a jackhammer on mega speed. "It's okay. I said might. Honestly, it's probably just a cold, which a doctor can't do anything about. It'll have to run its course."

He looked to her door, then the kitchen. "You sure? I can take you two to town to see the doc."

"Let's give it today. If she's not better tomorrow, then I'll call the doctor. For now, I'll take her temperature, and if she has a fever, I'll give her some Tylenol while you make her Nana's special drink."

He nodded and his heartbeat slowed. "I'll be right back."

Juniper retrieved the thermometer from the bathroom cabinet, sat by Gracie and smoothed her hair away from her forehead.

"I sick."

"I know, why didn't you tell me?" Juniper asked.

Gracie sniffled and wiped her nose with her knuckle. "I good help. Don't want bed."

Juniper checked Gracie's temp to discover a low-grade fever.

"I fever?"

"Yes."

"TV?"

Juniper smiled. "I'm sure Hudson will be happy to roll the television into your room if you're a good girl and remain in bed."

"I do."

Hudson returned with a mug and bag. He handed her the cup and sat on the other side of the bed from Juniper. "I have something special to me that I want you to borrow until you feel better." He pulled out the stuffed horse Juniper had made him after his mother died.

Her throat tightened at the sight of the worn-out cloth and yarn. He'd carried it around with him everywhere he'd gone for months. Juniper had looked for that horse a few times over the years but never found it. She'd thought he'd thrown it away.

"This is a special horse. It helps with all kinds of illnesses."

Gracie took it and snuggled it under her neck tight. "Horsey."

"It helps with itchy throats, sniffly noses and something called homesickness."

Had Hudson taken that with him to college, to New York? Had he been homesick? Why didn't he come home then? Because of his father's threats. Juniper took a deep breath of realization. For as much as she'd suffered from him leaving, he'd suffered as much for going.

Gracie didn't pay attention to another word. She abandoned her drink that smelled of peppermint and vanilla and snuggled down in her bed with the horse in one arm and her teddy in the other and shut her eyes.

"Where was that horse kept? How did you find it?" Juniper asked, her voice wobbling.

"I didn't have to look for it. That horse has been with me everywhere I've traveled since I left the farm. It kept me company in many hotel rooms sitting on my nightstand as I slept. You might think I ran from here and never thought about this place or of you, but that's not true. I thought of the farm and you every day. I might not have returned, but I never forgot."

"Forgot what?"

"That this place is the only place on Earth I've ever felt happy and loved."

Chapter Twelve

Hudson moved the papers from Juniper's lap and covered her in a blanket to take a nap, then went to check on Gracie. She still slept, but he worried her cheeks had turned a deeper shade of pink, so he rinsed out a small washcloth and pressed it to her forehead.

He could feel the heat from her face and thought to wake up Juniper to demand they take her to the doctor, but he'd probably be overreacting. What did he know about caring for little kids? He'd barely even seen one in the last decade or more.

The poor horse with one eye missing and the felt worn almost bare remained in Gracie's arms next to her teddy bear. They looked like they belonged together. His muscles were tight with worry at the tiny little thing under her pink-and-turquoise quilt Nana had no doubt made for her.

His heart tugged at the thought of how much Nana must've loved this little girl. How did she open up like that to everyone in the world? The woman loved everyone deeply. An ache formed in his chest. He tried to rub it free, but it remained. It settled deep inside.

Rain tapped at the window, reminding him of what a gloomy day it was outside. Another good reason to take a break from hard labor. However, without the physical exercise, his mind wandered into places it didn't need to go.

He took Gracie's little hand and held it, willing her to feel better. This had been planned as a two-week vacation to visit and help out at the farm because he knew he owed it to his nana. Now he found himself here for over a month, and at the bedside of little Gracie. A little one that had stolen his heart with her first hug. How would he walk away?

He smoothed the strands of golden hair plastered to her forehead in sweat. If he could be sick instead of her, he'd volunteer. How could God do things like allow kids to be sick and adults to be mean and the world to be cruel?

Yet here, in this room, peace didn't begin to describe the world around him. He'd forgotten how much love and fulfillment he'd experienced in this house, except when his father would decide to take a break from work long enough to rip him from here and drag him to some foreign place with the promise of time together and a real vacation, but it was always a lie. His father would use him to show off his faux happy family to some big businessman to finish a deal.

A tiny moan sounded from Gracie. Worry drove him to pull up the chair from the corner and sit by her side to wait for her to wake up, but the sound of the rain and the dim light made his eyes heavy. How did parents do it? If his stomach knotted at the sight of Gracie, what did a real parent go through watching their kids suffer?

He shifted in his chair to remain awake and keep a watchful eye on her, but his eyes closed, and he drifted off listening to the tap-tap-tap of the rain.

"Hey, you're going to have a kink in your neck." Juniper's voice startled him awake in what he thought was a few seconds, but he looked up and discovered everything had gone into night mode outside.

He scanned the area and found his hand still holding Gracie's. He slipped free and touched her cheeks.

"Fever broke—she's only sleeping. You've been in here all afternoon. I didn't have the heart to wake you, but that poor neck of yours was cranked to the side."

Relief flooded him. His muscles, all except for his neck, relaxed. He scrubbed his face and felt the stubble erupting like sprouts of weeds in a garden. "Sorry 'bout that. Guess we need to get back to work."

"About that." Juniper removed the washcloth and took it to the bathroom, then waved him to the door. "County meeting is day after tomorrow. I'll need to get everything ready to present. Would you mind listening to the speech I plan to give to the residents and board?"

"Sure, I'd be happy to. Why don't I make a pot of coffee and we can work for a couple hours."

"Already made. One cream, no sugar, waiting for you in the living room." Juniper winked. That wink toyed with his awareness that he'd have to leave her behind in a few days. Part of him wished he could push that county meeting out so he'd have an excuse to stay, but he needed to get back to work or their company would lose money. He couldn't expect Mark to start a new project on his own considering his condition.

For the first time in years, he didn't worry about a corporate takeover or bad business dealings. Strange how his attitude had been diluted by the false promise of forever comfort and happiness at the farm. But for how long? He was his father's son. Boredom would take over and he'd flee as fast as his father had abandoned his family.

They settled on the couch where she had several sheets of handwritten notes.

He wanted to help, but he also wished he could take the farm out of the equation and convince her to follow him back to New York City. Would she go if he asked her to? Did he have a right to insert himself into their lives like that? Gracie hadn't caused him any anger or resentment, and he thought he wanted to keep her in his life forever, but maybe that was because he didn't feel the need to mold her into his son that wouldn't disappoint him. Maybe not having babies of his own could make him a better man for raising children.

"Do you want more children?" he blurted before he even realized the words he'd put out there.

Her mouth dropped open and her eyes went shock-wide. "Ah, don't know. Why?"

He retreated from his question and pointed to the paper. "No reason. I'd be happy to give the speech if you want. I've got a lot of experience in that department. I know how to win over an audience."

"No thanks. This is my fight. My plan." Juniper lifted the paper, looked at it for a second, then lowered it back to her lap. "Wait, why did you ask if I wanted more children? Do you want children?"

"Not of my own. I wouldn't do that to a poor child."

"But Gracie… I can tell you're fond of her." Juniper sat still as a fence post.

"Of course. She's a special girl, who wouldn't adore her?" He realized his stupid question and added, "What man in his right mind, that is."

"You think you could have a child like Gracie but not your own." Juniper pressed her lips together and shook her head. "A child is a child."

"No, it's different for a man like my father or me to have a son. He needed me to be his person, the one who took over his empire, and I let him down. His anger made a constant appearance each time I disappointed him. A father to a little girl is different, especially a little girl who isn't my biological child. Listen, I'd like to visit and see you and Gracie, and maybe one day, if you want…" His voice cracked like a teenager after a day of screaming on roller coasters at Six Flags.

"If I want what?" Juniper asked, obviously nudging him to say more.

He inhaled and let out his breath, willing the words to form. His fingers messed with the fringe of the Afghan slung over the back of the couch. "You both could move to New York, closer to me. I mean, I'd pay for you both to live there. And who knows, maybe we might be able to figure out something between us."

"Ha!"

Her response wasn't what he'd hoped for. "What do you mean by ha?"

"I mean, you want me and Gracie in your life as some way for you to keep a connection with the life here at the farm without committing to living here or living this life. You want your cake and brownies and cookies, and you want them decorated, wrapped and delivered, too."

"I don't know what all that means, but I can tell I've offended you. Which was not my intention." Hudson patted the back of the couch several times as if to beat the dust out of the fabric, then stood up and paced the room. "Juniper, I'm not good at saying how I feel."

His insides twisted, tangled and tightened, but he knew he'd opened this hope chest of emotions Juniper had held on to for so long that he owed her more than a half promise. "I mean, I like you. My hope is that you'll move to New York so we can get to know each other better and see what happens. I know you want to start this hippotherapy program on the farm. We could still do that, but I need to be in New York to run my company. We could come here for vacation to check on things but run it remotely."

"You want me to uproot my life for a man who might have feelings for me that he can't even express and cause my daughter who needs stability and normalcy to move all the way to another state far from here with honking horns and pollution and millions of people. Only to return to the only home Gracie knows for sporadic vacations. Not to mention the fact that I'd be abandoning the hippotherapy program that is going to help Gracie. Does that about sum it up?"

He paced the floor. "No. I mean yes, but it wouldn't be like that."

"What would it be like, Hudson? Would it be that you work eighty hours a week and want me to remain at home waiting for you to bless me with your presence?"

Rejection stung, and he didn't like it. "If you don't want to accept my invitation, all you have to do is say so. You don't have to be rude."

"Invitation? You told me I should turn over the farm to you and abandon my life here so that I can be your security horse while you make a name for yourself to show your father that you're not a loser who chose to do his own business rather than to take over his. You don't want me because you like me, Hudson. You want me so you can have everything that makes you happy without having to work at it." She stood up with a huff, the pages wrinkled in her hand.

"That's not what I'm saying. Don't you understand that I care about you and Gracie?"

She paused at the doorway to the kitchen. "News flash, Hudson. I'm not a teenager willing to give up everything to make you happy. I have my daughter and my own life. I won't let you or anyone else take that away from me."

"I don't want to take anything away from you. I want to give you and Gracie everything and I have the means to do so, so why won't you let me?"

Juniper shook her head. The way her eyes drifted to the floor and her cheeks went tight told him he'd greatly disappointed her, upset her, but he couldn't understand why. "I thought you were starting to make a change. You were going to see what was important in life and do the right thing. I guess I should've known you'd only ever do the right thing for Hudson."

"You're accusing me of not wanting to fight, but you walk away when I'm trying to explain how I feel."

She tossed her hands in the air and rounded on him. "I'm not walking away, I'm staying. You're the one who runs the minute you start feeling something. That was you fifteen years ago, and that's you today. And I'm a fool for trusting it could be any different. When I saw you with Gracie, I thought… I thought…"

"Thought what?"

"That you'd finally understood that you don't have to be the man who won't let people close to his heart for fear of losing them. Loss is part of life, but we have to grab on to what is here now and enjoy it while we can. Embrace each other as the gift God gave us."

He looked at Juniper, then glanced over his shoulder. "If God gives us the gift of each other, why does He take it away?"

Tears rolled down her cheeks. "That's funny. You really don't see the truth."

"Truth?"

"He's not taking anything away. You are. Your fear and your need to control everything around you. That's why you'll never be happy. In your drive to be nothing like your father, you've become him. A lonely and unhappy man who won't let anyone close to his heart."

Shimmering morning light cast a spectrum of color through the crystal lamp resting on the desk. Juniper sat looking over her notes as she heard the distant laughter of Gracie being tickled and chased by Hudson.

A churning stomach would be an understatement. More like a roaring eruption of hot trepidation seared her resolve. But she had no choice but to speak in front of everyone. The girl who liked being in the shadows more than in the spotlight had to face a room full of Willow Oaks residents and win them over. If Nana were here, she'd know the right thing to say to give her confidence. But she wasn't, and this had to be done.

With one more cleansing breath with a hint of cinnamon from the homemade potpourri in the crystal dish by her side, Juniper stood and checked herself in the mirror. The dress fit well, and the rose color made her hair and eyes stand out. Not that this would be a fashion show, but sometimes dressing up gave a person confidence. It had been a long time since she'd worn a dress. Besides church, there wasn't much reason to dress up.

After retying the fabric belt one last time, she lifted her chin and walked around the pile of kitchen tile yet to be installed and prepared to leave her home to face the world beyond the safety of the farm.

In the living room, Hudson stopped with one hand in the air midgallop with Gracie on his back.

"Go horsey!" Gracie yelled.

"Look at your mom. Doesn't she look beautiful?" He slid Gracie from his back, and she gasped.

"Princess."

"Yes, she does look like a princess." Hudson remained on his knees, his mouth open and gaze transfixed on her. She wanted to squirm under his attention, but she refused to let him know how much he affected her. Since their conversation the other night, she knew exactly where they stood, which was on the other side of life's fence from each other.

"We should go. We don't want to be late. Go get your jacket—it might be cold in the building."

Gracie ran to her room like a good girl, all smiles and sunshine and satisfaction. Too bad her world would crumble soon. Juniper should've stayed firm about keeping them apart, but it was tough with them near each other all the time. No, that was not why she'd let him around her daughter. Hudson hadn't been the only one lying to himself. She'd done the same thing when she believed what she wanted to about him instead of the glaring truth.

He stood and approached. His fingers tugged at hers, but she balled her fist. "You can go after we show a united front at the meeting. I'm sure you're anxious to return to your company."

"Why won't you talk to me?" Hudson didn't give up. He pried her fist open, held her hand and stepped closer. Her heart beat fast and loud. Space, she needed space.

"After the meeting, once Gracie's down for the night, we need to discuss what the future has for us," Hudson continued. "I've been doing a lot of thinking, and maybe we can just take things slow."

Juniper knew she couldn't deal with this right now. Too much on the line, and she needed to focus, so she pulled her hand free and grabbed her own jacket. "Fifteen years is slow enough. It's time for me to move on. Gracie and I have plans, and so do you. Neither is wrong, they just don't align, so we both need to face facts—there's a reason we never worked out."

Gracie raced by them and waited by the truck for Hudson to put her in and then take his place in the driver's seat.

She was thankful for a chatting and squealing little girl who covered the uncomfortable silence with songs and clapping. For as many words as she couldn't say, she could sing twenty times more.

"You know, I've been thinking. We have other options. I've been researching equine therapies, and like you mentioned it can be useful for so many other populations—post-traumatic stress disorder, stress management, anxiety, depression—"

"Stop. Please, just stop. I've done my research, and I've already established a budget to include a therapist, and I'm being certified as an aide to help with the program. Grant proposals are all ready to present, and the documentation is set. I need to focus on what's coming straight ahead of me. You want to talk, fine, after this is over."

He only nodded his affirmation and kept driving.

At the sight of town, her stomach rolled, and

her pulse did a trot. Her breath came in short, tight bursts.

"You've got this." He patted her shoulder in an awkward bro kind of way, and she wanted more. She wanted him to pull her in and hold her tight.

He parked and shut off the engine, and she knew none of that would be possible. She was on her own, the way she'd be from this day forward.

"You stay with Gracie, so I don't have to worry, and I'll give my speech and plead our case."

"I can help."

"You are. I don't trust anyone else but you with her." The irony of her words wasn't lost on her, but for now, she had a mission to focus on, so she wrenched open her door, hotfooted it into the courthouse, followed the signs to the county board office and walked into a large room housing rows of chairs and a long table at the far end with county commissioners facing the crowd.

She spotted Mindi and thought to ask her to watch Gracie, but Hudson kept her calm. Now wasn't the time to pull them apart. Besides, Mindi sat next to Pastor John. She didn't want to interrupt that big move in the relationship direction.

Her mind raced with thoughts of running or hiding under something, but when Hudson arrived and directed her past the hundred or so people to the front row where seats were reserved for them, she had no choice but to follow through with her plan.

A few forms. That's all it should've taken to start this business. "Do you want to pray?"

Hudson's words startled her, but she swallowed down her wayward thoughts of a changed man and offered her best smile. "Already been praying all the way here."

"Then you'll be just fine."

It turned into standing-room only, and when she spotted the T-shirt on ten people, all friends of Ace Gatlin, that read Save Our Town from Criminals and Misfits, she knew for sure he'd been the cause of all this drama.

The county manager called the meeting to order, and the secretary announced the first person on the agenda. After four other people got up and made speeches on the topic and answered questions, and a vote was taken, it was three nos and one yes. Not feeling positive, she couldn't help but glance at Hudson, who nodded and leaned in to whisper, "You've got this. A change of a road name is nothing like offering a service to people in your community."

"Next on the agenda is Ms. Juniper Keller. Please come forward to explain your proposal for hippopotamus therapy."

The room erupted in laughter, but education would be her first item to address. "That is hippotherapy, which is a form of equine therapy or therapy with horses."

"Your horse needs therapy? Wait, you don't even have a horse no more." Mr. Chester, dressed in one of the anti-hippotherapy shirts, mocked her.

Ace shot him a sideways glance. The man was gruff at times and wanted her home, but appeared to hush the man on her behalf. Surprising if Hudson's suspicions about his father working with Ace were true.

The county manager pounded his mallet faster than her pulse hammered her temple. Or was that anger? "You're out of order."

"Sorry, I just didn't understand how someone could run a horse program with no horse." Mr. Chester elbowed Ace in the ribs, but the man straightened to his six-foot-three, football stature.

"I'll be addressing that if I'm given the opportunity." She cleared her throat. She'd stand here and take all the hits, if that was what she had to do to make a better life for her daughter. Because Juniper was all Gracie had in this world. As her mother, she needed to do everything she could to give her the best life, and living in Hudsonville wouldn't be an option any longer.

Mr. Chester lifted his cane in the air. "We don't need no riffraff in our town, though."

Ace turned to Mr. Chester and said, "Let the woman speak. It's her right."

Juniper didn't understand the conundrum of Ace Gatlin, but now wasn't the time to dig into his issues, because she needed to focus.

Mindi stood up and cleared her throat. "If you two don't mind, I'd like to hear Juniper Keller's proposal."

She so appreciated her friend and confidante at that moment. Juniper cleared her throat and the room fell quiet, too quiet, and all her preparation jumbled in her brain and her words misfired. She couldn't grasp a train of thought. Only the dozens of eyes staring at her.

Chapter Thirteen

Hudson snuggled Gracie into his side. With her earphones in place and her iPad in her lap, she wouldn't likely have any sort of tantrum, he hoped, because he wanted his full attention on Juniper and her presentation. Not that Mr. Chester gave her much opportunity to present her case.

In retrospect, Hudson should've done a full background check and figured out why Ace Gatlin was against this therapy program and why he wanted the farm so badly, but after his father disappeared overseas, he figured he could deal whatever came from local issues. And he had to respect Juniper's wishes to let her handle things on her own. It wasn't easy to stand by and not do what he did best: dig up dirt on his opponent to bury him under.

Hudson's blood simmered under his cool facade at the constant interruptions. Mr. Chester should be taught some manners, but somehow normal business tactics didn't seem proper in Willow Oaks.

Whispers hopped from ear to ear around the room until they arrived at the elderly lady at his side who looked up at him, opened her mouth, but then shut it and faced forward.

Wise choice.

He wanted to get up there and defend Juniper and tell the room how brilliant she was and how he now saw her real worth beyond her smile.

The knight-in-shining-armor complex rode in with a vengeance, but he knew he couldn't break his promise, or he'd risk alienating Juniper even more than he already had since he'd arrived.

And he had deserved her mistrust and anxiety over his presence. He'd all but kicked them both out on the front lawn upon his arrival, upset Gracie and Juniper, and then tried to run the entire place as if he knew best, when she'd taken care of the farm and his grandmother all these years.

"Well, go on, then," Mr. Chester grumbled.

Juniper shuffled the notes in front of her and cleared her throat again. Hudson wanted to run up there and take her into his arms and hug her distress away.

"This program will provide a much-needed service to so many in our community," she said in a shaky voice.

Mr. Chester stood as if he'd noticed a weakness and hoped to push his way through it. "You mean the one child that needs this? You want to take county funds to help yourself, not the community."

"No, there are so many more beyond our town that—"

"Now you want to bring in strangers and with it menace and crime to our safe homes." Mrs. Chester joined in on the attack. They were the town conspiracy theorists from what he remembered. It wouldn't matter if Juniper stood up there to give away free tickets to Paris, they would argue it would be a bad idea.

"No, it wouldn't be like that." She bit her bottom lip and shifted between feet.

Hudson stiffened. Gracie patted his arm, soothing his temper, but how long would he be able to sit and listen to their fellow town residents make snide remarks to a woman Hudson couldn't help but want to protect?

Nana would tell him to smother his rudeness with kindness, but Hudson had already proven he was never going to be as good as Nana.

Juniper curled the edge of the paper. Her mouth opened and closed twice.

How long would he be forced to witness this struggle without taking action? Not a moment longer. He cleared his throat and was about to stand despite his promise when her gaze snapped to him.

An epic fifteen-year war battled in her eyes

until she lifted her chin and said, "And it won't be only for children. We have people in this town who will be able to use equine therapy. People like Ms. Johnson, who spoke earlier about needing someone to take meals to the people who are homebound because she suffers from anxiety since her car accident, or Mr. Ranger for his balance since his stroke."

Hudson let out a long breath and a hint of warmth filled him at the realization she had listened to him about offering beyond developmental and physical clients, and in an indirect way, he could offer her some sort of assistance even if behind the scenes. Not something he'd ever experienced before, but it felt good just the same.

"As much as I appreciate your willingness to support others in our town, two or three are not enough to constitute a necessity, especially when there are services available one county over," Ace said. He spoke in a diplomatic tone, but Hudson's legs burned with the need to stand and tell the man to sit down and be quiet.

"There are others who experience both mental and physical challenges that will benefit from this program. From leg injuries to attention deficit disorder to post-traumatic stress disorder."

Ace about-faced and walked to the back of the room as if he couldn't sit still another moment.

A fire lit Juniper's eyes. She lifted her chin and

abandoned her papers to take center stage in the room. "Who here wants a place for your sons, daughters, nephews, nieces, parents, brothers and sisters to go when they return from fighting for our country? Who doesn't want to provide services to children with speech issues, socialization challenges, sensory and emotional needs? The elderly facing the aftermath of strokes and heart attacks."

"Sitting on a horse isn't going to save everyone from every problem. Trust me. There's some wounds that no amount of horse therapies can heal." A vein in the side of Ace's temple pulsed.

Hudson saw such pain and resentment oozing from this man. A man who'd obviously gone through something because he didn't look anything like the boy from childhood. His once silly disposition and crooked grin had been replaced by a scowl and harsh words as bitter as Ms. Ranger's lemon tartlets.

"No, but it'll offer so much to so many. You can view all the benefits on the website I've listed on the handout." Juniper pointed to the papers abandoned on the floor or in purses around the room.

Several people pulled out their phones and the pamphlets, showing she'd won over a possible few, but was it enough?

Mr. Chester chuckled, but there was no lightness to his voice. "How can a woman on her own who couldn't even hold a marriage together run a program like this?"

Blood pulsed through Hudson, and he shot up, leaving Gracie on the chair beside him. "No reason to get personal."

"Although Mr. Chester is out of line with his comment, he isn't wrong. She isn't a business tycoon or even someone with a business degree. She's not equipped to face the demands of such a project," Ace said.

Hudson met the county manager's gaze with a warning glower, edging him to intervene with a smack of his gavel. "Personal insults will not be tolerated."

Gracie tugged at Hudson's sleeve until he sat down beside her, and she curled into his side, her face scrunched with warning, so he lifted her into his lap and held her as she played on her iPad.

The crowd's whispers turned into back-of-the-school-bus chatter.

"I'm just saying..." Juniper shuffled the papers again and Hudson could see her face and neck tinge red. "I'm saying that..."

"Call for a vote, and let the people decide," Ace ordered as if commanding troops into battle.

The gavel hammered three times until the audience settled back into whispers and points and headshakes.

The county manager's lips tightened, and he clasped his hands in front of him. "If there isn't any more information, I'd like to open the room to additional questions. We've heard from both Mrs. Keller and the opposing objections of Mr. and Mrs. Chester and Mr. Gatlin. Are there any others who wish to speak?"

Mindi rose and looked down at Pastor John, who joined her. "We both would like to extend our support to Mrs. Keller."

Pastor John nodded.

"Thank you, Mindi and Pastor John. If no one else has anything to say, I would like to add to the discussion." The county manager sat forward, setting his gavel down on the table. "I knew Mrs. Kenmore, Hudson's grandmother, for most of my life, so I want to ask the audience to consider who owned that land. Mrs. Kenmore was an outstanding member of our community. She took food to shut-ins, drove people two towns over for doctor appointments when they couldn't drive themselves. She single-handedly ran our spring festival, did church outreach, ran a women's Bible study, served as treasurer on the Ladies of Wisdom board and president of the Red Hat Society. She also taught knitting and sewing, and so much more I can't list it all. In the end, this was her land and I think we should all take that into consideration as we vote."

"Amen, County Manager Richards," a lady in a purple hat with red ribbon hollered.

Gracie leaned into Hudson's chest, and he knew he couldn't allow this vote to go forward without saying something. He'd kept his promise, mostly, not to interfere with her fight, but with the question of what Nana would do lingering in the air, a passage in the Bible struck him. This wasn't a fight over him keeping his land and making money. He kissed Gracie's floral-smelling, soft hair, lifted her into his arms and stood. The room fell silent.

"We should allow Mr. Kenmore to speak. He owns half the land," Ace announced.

"I own the other half," Juniper said.

"Juniper's correct. Nana left the land and house to us both, but I do have something I believe she'd want to share here today."

"Go ahead." County Manager Richards tipped his gavel toward Hudson.

"Matthew 19:14 states, 'But Jesus said, Suffer little children, and forbid them not to come unto me: for of such is the kingdom of heaven.'"

Ace threw his hands up in the air. "What's that supposed to mean? We can quote Bible verses all day, but this isn't a church, it's a public meeting."

"This isn't about church. It's about doing the right thing. The county manager asked what Nana would want."

Ace pushed up his sleeves as if he'd planned on taking this debate outside. "How would you know? You've not been around forever and a week."

"I know that my grandmother left this land to both Juniper and me for a reason, because Nana never did anything without a purpose. Unfortunately, I didn't know what that reason was until now."

"What reason's that?" the county manager asked.

"She wanted to make me see something I never could see before. A life beyond the next big deal. A life beyond riches but a life with purpose. Like the innocence of a child who doesn't look at themselves as important and who gives with true heart and soul. Gracie here is that child. She and her mother have taught me things I never learned in college or in the corporate world. I've learned about gifts beyond money and status. I've learned about the gifts of joy and happiness and purpose," Hudson said.

The county manager nodded.

Ace grunted.

Hudson cleared his throat. "Ace, you stated you worried that Juniper didn't get a business degree, but I have. I can guarantee that this business will have the benefit of the academic background and decade of solid business decisions that have taken me from poor to prosperous. But I can tell you now that I'm not the one who possesses the skills to make this equine and hippotherapy program a success. Juniper and her daughter have the knowledge, the work ethic, the drive and the hearts to make this a huge opportunity not only to serve this county but to bring in new business and boost the local economy. Think about it—people will need to eat and shop while in town, and some will even come to spend the night at our inn."

He faced Juniper, who stood with shaking hands and tears in her eyes, and he knew he'd broken his promise. And based on her tight lips and narrowed gaze, he had to face the fact that she'd never believe he'd ever be anything more than a liar and a man with a heart of stone.

Juniper saw it. The love in Hudson's eyes—even if he couldn't face it, he did feel it. She thought she'd run and hug him for his words and support, but she wanted the last word at the town hall meeting. Not because she wanted to win an argument or because she wanted to show Hudson she didn't need him. It was as if Nana sent her a message from Heaven, helping her find her voice, her truth. "God loves everyone. And everyone is worthy of God's love. Shouldn't we make decisions based on glorifying Him?"

The strangest thing happened at her declaration. Mr. and Mrs. Chester quieted, and Ace sat down and didn't utter another word. That man had a tortured, vacant look on his face and appeared to be stunned into silence. Juniper only hoped that whatever ailed him, he'd come to her program to find help.

She'd spent hours poring over the Bible looking for wisdom, but she hadn't realized the one thing that mattered—God loved her and she was deserving. It didn't matter that she didn't have a business degree or that she had a failed marriage. She had a right to work and to be loved. Not only His love but she deserved someone who would treasure her the way she would cherish him.

"If that's all, you may take your seat." The county manager leaned over, covering his mic, and whispered to the person at his side.

Juniper took her seat next to Hudson, who tucked Gracie between them and put his arm around them both. Her heart pitter-pattered faster than Gracie's little feet across the wood floor in the mornings.

The town mumbled and whispered, but everyone fell silent when the board called for the official vote.

"Please, respond with your vote," the county manager said.

"Yes." The woman at the end spoke into her microphone. Her voice echoed through the room and into Juniper's ears and heart.

"Yes." Another and then another, and by the end of the row, it was unanimous.

Juniper jumped up and wrapped her arms around Hudson, who took her and swung her around, then stopped and pulled a clapping Gracie into their side.

Hudson's eyes reflected pure joy like Juniper had never seen from him. "You did it."

"We did it." She corrected him. "All of us."

"I do?" Gracie asked.

Hudson tickled her tummy. "You do best."

She giggled and squirmed all the way to the truck but dozed the minute they'd pulled from the parking lot. Hudson took Juniper's hand and kissed her knuckles, sending the jolt of a dozen espressos through her. "I know I don't have the right, but I'm so proud of you. Listen, you're going to rock this program, and I was stupid to have ever doubted you. By the way, James lost the best thing that ever happened to him, and you deserve so much better. You're a ray of sunshine in a dark world."

They pulled into the farm and Gracie raced inside to grab her favorite Chutes and Ladders game.

"We play? We play?" Gracie bounced up and down.

"I'm game." Hudson removed his suit jacket

and draped it over the back of the chair. "After I make some celebratory hot chocolate."

They settled in together around the coffee table sipping hot chocolate and moving characters up and down the board while laughter filled the room with the sound she'd missed since Nana had passed.

The house felt like a home again. The home she'd missed when she'd gone away with James, but now she would keep it for Gracie to grow up with happy memories the way Juniper had.

Hudson toyed with Juniper's fingers, distracting her from the game and filling her heart with hope. Crickets sang a lullaby, and Gracie faded, her eyelids falling along with her body into him. He scooped her up and carried her to bed, slid the horse under the covers on one side of her and the bear on the other, then tucked her in like she slept in a pink-and-turquoise cocoon, just the way she liked it. After he flicked on the nightlight, he turned and looked at Juniper in a new way. Hope sparked again in the dim light, taking her breath and making it whirl inside her like a funnel of emotions.

This man, the self-proclaimed horrible man who didn't ever want children, had slid into the dad role without either of them realizing it. "You're amazing," she whispered in the hallway.

"I think you're the amazing one. Look at all

you've done." He moved in, caressing her cheek and eyeing her with an adoring gaze that caused those hummingbirds to flutter in her belly.

"We've done." She longed to show him how much he'd changed and the man he'd become in a short time on the farm, but there were no words.

He ran a hand through his hair and stepped away from her. "I should go. We've got lots of work to finish up before the horses and the therapist can arrive. I'll finish the tiling in the kitchen tomorrow."

Before she could stop him, he hotfooted it to the front door. "I need to figure a few things out."

Juniper wasn't sure what he meant, but she knew what she'd hoped. That he'd decided to stick around awhile longer. But was that a good thing?

She went to bed but sleep only came in fitful dreams of lost opportunities and broken hearts. Sometime in the night, she heard Nana whispering to her in a dream, "Take another chance. Tell him how you feel."

She jolted upright and searched the room but only found emptiness in the morning sun. The *Little Einsteins* song blared from the living room. Her pulse triple-tapped with the thought of Hudson already sitting by Gracie's side. With a jolt of Hud-adrenaline, she flew out of bed, brushed her teeth, primped a little more than a farm girl should and raced to the living room, but there was no sign of Hudson.

Gracie buried deep in her show meant there would be a good twenty minutes before breakfast and morning routine needed to start.

Take another chance. Tell him how you feel.

Her mouth went Sahara Desert dry. Could she open her heart again only to have it crushed? She flew out the front door before she could change her mind and found Hudson preparing hay for the soon-to-arrive horses, his muscles tight from working for what could've been hours.

The aroma of damp earth, straw and lost dreams lingered. Hudson paused and set the pitchfork aside, removed his gloves and looked up through his disheveled hair. "I hope I didn't wake you. I've been up all night, though, thinking."

She swallowed a cow-sized lump. "About?"

Her breath caught somewhere between her lungs and her dreams of a happily-ever-after with Hudson.

"I've spent my entire life avoiding a family, but apparently God and Nana had other plans for me." He chuckled and tossed his gloves to the ground. His gaze bounced from a stall—where he'd slept one night after his father had lost his temper and she brought him a blanket—to the loft where they'd shared their first kiss, and then settled on her. "I'm not worthy of you and Gracie, but I hope to be someday. That is, I spent all night convincing myself to leave and allow you an easier life without me, but I couldn't. I can't." He ran a hand through his hair, tossing the damp strands away from his face in that model way of his.

She sucked in a quick breath and took a brave step toward him. "You don't have to go. You don't have to stay. It's your choice, and you can take whatever time you need to figure out what you want in life. I wanted to protect Gracie—"

"So do I. That's why I almost left. The way you were yesterday took my breath away, to match the heart you already stole from me all those years ago, here in this barn. You've been a pillar of strength in such adversity. A woman who survived a broken marriage to a man who gambled away your hard work. You survived the loss of your parents, and you took care of my nana. Something I'll always remember. You were there when I wasn't, and there is no excuse for that, but that's what makes you special. Even now, you don't resent me for it. I'm sorry for so many things."

She closed the distance between them and placed her palm on his chest. "Don't. You have an amazing heart, one that is giving and true. You don't need to carry everything on your shoulders alone. No one can handle that much load. You're not responsible for what your father did to your mother or how he treated you. Hudson, you are your own man. Strong, smart, handsome, sweet."

"You think I'm handsome?" He winked.

"Don't deflect. You already know how good-looking you are physically. What you don't know is how good-looking you are on the inside."

Hudson shook his head. "I wish I could see myself the way you see me. The way you've shown me I can be. I didn't believe I could be a good father. How can I be with the example I grew up with…but I love that little girl, and…" His eyes misted, and it tugged her a step closer, but she paused. Could she let him back into her heart without there being a promise of tomorrow?

"What are you saying? I can handle you staying and figuring things out, but don't say you're staying for good, then run."

"At this moment, the only place I want to run is to you and Gracie. But I don't know what that looks like. I have a business in New York, and you have a home here. But I'd like to try."

A spark of connection turned over deep in her soul and caught fire. She saw the man standing in front of her she always wanted, the man who spoke with a soft voice but a strong will, a man tough yet kind, a man with a gentle touch.

She pressed her fingertips to his bottom lip and he let out a warm breath that caressed her skin.

As if he used his hidden key, he unlocked her heart and she trusted she deserved him. She wasn't some big shot in New York, but she had more to offer him than any of those models and actresses he'd dated, according to the papers.

"Juniper," he said in a deep, hoarse whisper.

"June Bug." She smiled and lifted up on her toes. "I'm your June Bug." In the same spot they'd kissed so many years ago, she pressed her lips to his, sending her pulse into a roaring thunder, her heart beating so hard and fast she thought it tried to leap from her chest to reach his.

They melded together into one person, as if they'd been torn apart for years and finally found their other half.

It wasn't a kiss of passion alone, but of reconnection, a welcome-home embrace.

When the kiss ended, he pulled her cheek to his chest and held her there as if he feared she'd float away if he let her go. She listened to his heart beat rapid and hard, making him feel alive and full of possibilities. "I don't know what happened, but I can't leave you. You or Gracie. I can't make any promises, but I'd like to stay longer with you and Gracie and see if we can figure something out."

She leaned back and looked up into his face

and saw the truth, his truth. He'd finally accepted that he belonged on the farm, and life would finally be perfect.

Chapter Fourteen

For a week, Hudson slept like he hadn't in years. Each morning, he raced to get to the house and make breakfast, finish up the inside renovations they'd agreed to, and all day he spent working to get ready for the grand opening. Today, they all climbed into the truck to drop off more flyers and pick up more supplies.

Juniper had found a physical therapist who'd wanted to be part of this new venture; the grants were rolling in, and for the first time in as long as Hudson could remember, he felt alive and happy.

Mark had even agreed for Hudson to work remotely. A trial to see if the arrangement would be effective with one travel day a month. That was all the time he could spare away from Juniper and Gracie. Not that he was even happy about that.

They rolled into a parking place in town and divided up their errands so they could make it back in time for Gracie's nap, which meant alone time with Juniper. The part of the day he looked forward to the most.

Ace swept the front walkway of the feedstore and grunted at him. "Not sure how things are gonna go moving forward, but she won. We'll see how it goes."

His words were laced with warning, but Hudson wouldn't allow the man to bait him into a foul mood. He understood bitterness and said a silent prayer for the man to have more than sadness and resentment in his life. In contrast to Ace, Mindi greeted him at the grocer with her normal cheerful smile and wave. "You work here, too?"

Mindi smiled. "Yep, saving for college. You know I couldn't go when I was younger because I was raising siblings, but it's never too late, right?"

"Right. I think that's great. Good for you." Hudson smiled. "Do you have the swirl lollipops in today?"

"I have some in the back. Ms. Ranger put them aside saying you'd want to come pick them up for Gracie. That little girl looks good. You've been good for them both."

"Thanks, I appreciate that. Any idea of something I might pick up special for Juniper, too?"

"Tulips?" She grinned conspiratorially.

"I think you were off about Juniper's favorite being tulips. My ladies are more about wildflowers. Must be something special I could give her, though."

"Can't think of anything but shiny and round."

Mindi winked and skittered away, leaving the seed of an idea in his head.

No, they weren't ready for that. They needed to figure some things out, and he wouldn't rush her, considering what she'd gone through with James. He'd be patient and kind like the Bible said love should be.

Love, that was still a frightening word, but he didn't run from it this time. After securing the lollipops, he put them in the glove box where Gracie wouldn't see them until reward time for cleaning her room or doing something outside her comfort zone.

He walked along the street, spotting Gracie playing in the town square with another child, and he stood back admiring how she'd opened up to the world so much recently. Hippotherapy would help her even more. Structure, dependability and a father would be the best thing for her.

Did he dare to believe he could ever truly have a place here for the rest of his days?

"You've really done it now. Gone and fell in love despite all my hard work."

His father's voice sucker punched him. Hudson swallowed and turned to see his father standing two feet from him, glowering with disapproval.

Hudson's palms slicked with sweat, so he wiped them down his pants, took a breath of courage and forced a calm to his voice he didn't feel. "I tried to call you back, but you never answered. Secretary said you were out of the country. What are you doing here?"

"I'm back and, as always, I'm here to keep you from ruining your life."

Hudson straightened and realized his father had shrunk, but his attitude had only grown. "I'm not you. This is the life for me. I spent too many years wasting my time trying to be the man you said I'd never be. Now I want to be the man I want to be."

"You ran once, you'll run again. You're just like me, so you might as well give up on this fantasy and take your rightful place by my side at Kenmore Enterprises." He scoffed and unbuttoned his custom suit jacket. The old man attempted to hide his age with Botox and surgery—he'd always been vain about his image, the opposite of Nana.

"I spent the last ten years thinking about what I'd say to you if I ever saw you again, but now I realize there isn't anything worth saying. You won't listen, and our relationship is poison, so you should go."

"I'm leaving as fast as I arrived. Thanks to my friends on the town council, I found out what's been going on, and I've put securities in place to make sure this insane project doesn't move forward. I'll tear down that old shack and put up a resort. You can run it, and we can merge our companies."

Hair on the back of Hudson's neck prickled. "Not interested."

"Oh, I think you'll be very interested." He shuffled closer, his bitter breath and spirit infecting the air around Hudson.

"Never. I'm no longer a young boy who can be manipulated. I won't be the man who destroys a family so he can have riches. The one thing I've realized over the years is that no matter how much money you have, you'll never be happy. Your future is bitter and cold, and I don't want to be you, Father."

"You're too much like your mother, romanticizing life. This is business, and I've waited a long time to destroy the place that stole my life for so long. My father died when I was young, leaving me to run the place. Forced to care for my mother and then a wife who tried to cage me and manipulate me into remaining when I'd worked so hard to escape. That place is poison."

"Let it go. You have everything you ever wanted, why destroy it now?"

"Because of you." He took out his handkerchief and wiped his face. Instead of removing his jacket in the hot sun, he'd rather stand there sweating and perfectly dressed.

"Why can't you let me be and leave us alone?"

"Because you're too much like your mother, and the minute something happens to that little girl, you'll die, too."

His words pounded his skull, but Hudson couldn't make them out. "What are you talking about?"

"You seriously don't remember? Thought that was always an act so you didn't have to talk about it. Your sister. Your baby sister."

Hudson shook his head, dislodging a memory or two. A cry, the smell of baby shampoo. It seared his skin, but he couldn't see anything. "What baby sister?"

"The one that died when you were four. The one that caused your mother to slip into a deep depression and never get out. The one I couldn't afford to save because I was so poor." His expression turned glacial. "And I won't let you fall apart when something happens to that little girl. I couldn't save your mother, but I can save you."

The thought of something happening to Gracie sent a chill through him that made his bones shiver.

"Someday you'll wake up and realize your place is by my side. My empire will remain in our family, and we'll build upon it."

Hudson's feet pointed in two different directions, one toward Gracie and one out of town. No, he wouldn't let his father's fears take everything away from him again. He shook his head, his fear draining from his body and replaced by sorrow. "When is it enough?"

"When I know I'll never have to return to begging for scraps to keep my family alive. I didn't have a choice but to be stuck there for decades. I won't allow my son to die on that farm like the rest of my family. I heard you already decided to take a step back from your own company. As your father, I won't allow it. You'll return, and next week we'll start a merger so that we'll finally be one company, a family company."

"We've never been a family. My family is Juniper and Gracie. We're done here." Hudson about-faced and headed to the park.

"I'll burn it to the ground. I'll bury that stupid horse program under so much bureaucratic paperwork it never begins, and I'll bleed your existing company until it's barely alive, take it over so you have no external income and then you'll come begging for a job."

"Stop. Let me go and have the life I want." Hudson gritted his teeth and closed his mind to his father's threats.

"I'm only going to say this once. You come work for me, and I'll leave the farm alone. Don't and that lady and child will be on the streets, and you'll have no choice but to take your rightful place at Kenmore Enterprises." He took four steps before he rounded on Hudson once more. "You have twenty-four hours to report to New York. Don't bother telling that girl why you're leaving. She'll only try to talk you out of it, and she's like your mother. She'll never leave the farm because she loves it more than you."

"I won't," Hudson said with the most authoritative tone he could muster. Despite all the board meetings he'd attended, all the companies he'd taken over, sold or restored, he had never wavered. But his father always made him feel like that small boy hiding from him in the barn.

"If you don't report to my office by this time tomorrow, I'll make a call and the lawyers will fight for my right to that property, and you know I'll win, or at least keep the fight going on long enough neither of you will survive. But let's face it, the courts would see that I'm her only living son, after all."

Hudson fell against the truck knowing his father would use injunctions, stop orders, bribery and anything else he could to get what he wanted. The one thing Hudson had managed to stay away from all his life now threatened to ruin all his hard work. His father finally had the ammo he'd carefully kept away all along, and he wouldn't hesitate to fire.

In that moment, he remembered why he'd left the farm all those years ago. His father had made the same threat then, but this time was different. This time, he'd have no choice but to work for his father because Nana, the one person in the world that could keep his father in check, was gone.

Hudson would have no option but to leave, but he couldn't tell Juniper why. She'd try to change his mind. She hadn't understood the consequences fifteen years ago, and she wouldn't understand them now.

His heart slashed in two, and he knew he'd leave half here in Willow Oaks with the woman he'd loved his entire life and his special almost-daughter.

They climbed into the truck and Hudson handed Gracie a lollipop for no reason. Juniper raised an eyebrow at him.

"She was good, why not?" he said, his words sounding short and holding no warmth.

A quiet car ride home unsettled Juniper. Hudson white-knuckled the steering wheel and his lips were pressed into a thin line, eyes straight ahead.

Firecrackers exploded over her skin.

Something had changed while they were in town, but she couldn't understand how anything ignited such a turnaround in demeanor in only an hour.

She bit her tongue, not wanting to ask while in

the car with Gracie still licking on her lolly with a smile, clueless to the war raging behind Hudson's eyes. Whatever it was, it was big.

She ushered Gracie into the house for her nap and then went to find Hudson to discuss what was bothering him, but he wasn't in the house or the field or the barn. The open door to his apartment made her stomach drop. He never went in there except to sleep. He even worked in the house.

With shaking hands she grabbed the railing, ignoring the sound of a loud zipper, the kind on a suitcase. Her legs wobbled under her, and she had to gather all her strength to make it to the top. Certainly, he wouldn't leave again. Not after he'd promised he wanted her and Gracie in his life.

She nudged open the door to find Hudson lifting the suitcase he'd bought in town off the bed and his duffel from the desk.

"Were you even going to say goodbye?" she asked, her voice cracking on the word *goodbye* because she saw the truth wheeling toward her. She'd seen that same look in the car fifteen years ago, when he'd fled the farm to protect her. "Tell me what he did."

Hudson stalled but kept his gaze trained on the cracked wooden floor. "Who?" He didn't give her a chance to answer before he threw the strap of the duffel over his shoulder and headed for the door, but she stepped into his path.

"I won't make it so easy for you this time." The memories of him walking away choked her, but she cleared the pain and knew this time she'd have her say first.

"You promised you'd never leave without a word again, that you wouldn't break Gracie's heart, my heart." The tears slid down her cheeks, but she didn't care about being brave; she cared about fighting with every tool she could throw at him.

"I have to go." He cleared his throat, then grabbed her hands and closed the space between them. "Trust me, it's for the best."

She yanked her hands free. "That's what James said."

"I'm not James."

"And I'm not your mother." She saw the flicker of pain tighten his jaw, but she needed to say it. "You're not your father and I'm not your mother. We're not destined to hate each other and live a miserable life ultimately ending in my death when you walk out."

"What about Gracie's?"

"What?"

"Nothing." He turned away, but not before she noticed the glint of tears pooling in the corner of his eyes.

"I'm stronger than that, and you're better than that. You want to be here, I see it in your face. You don't want to go."

"I'm leaving," he whispered.

"Why? Why do you have to go?" She willed him to tell her the truth.

"It doesn't matter."

"There, I see it."

He glanced at her face but then looked over her head. "What?"

"You." She cupped his cheeks and forced him to see her. "The protective, 'I have to save the world and everyone around me' Hudson. You don't have to be that person this time. Not alone."

His jaw clicked and his nostrils flared. "It's more complicated than that. If he..."

He pried her hands from his cheeks and grabbed the handle of his bag, but she wouldn't relent.

"Go ahead, finish. Your father did what?"

"You don't know him like I do. You live with faith and dreams, but I live in cruel reality. He'll ruin you, me, everyone I care about. This entire place will be lost."

"Then we'll fight together." She stepped into his space again, not allowing him to look away.

"There's no fighting him," Hudson ground out.

"Even today, despite the fact that you're a grown man, he has all the power and you're still the young boy hiding from him in the barn." She touched his shoulder. He flinched, but she willed him to hear her words.

"Not fair." He shrugged her hand away and rolled his suitcase forward, but she shot in front of the door, arms outstretched.

"Fight, Hudson. Fight with me. Fight with Gracie."

His lips pressed together, and his gaze darted around like a jumping bean. He opened his mouth, then closed it, then lifted her, set her aside and headed down the stairs, the wheels of his suitcase hitting each step with a resounding thud as if the Little Drummer Boy played his exit march.

A fierce wind picked up and tossed the unlatched barn doors open. Hay swirled and twirled around them, but she didn't slow until she reached him again. "Stop. You can't keep running. If you run away again, I'll never let you back into our lives. Do you hear me?"

"I won't have a reason to return." His voice and expression froze her heart. "The farm is yours. It's what you wanted, right? It's your way or no way at all. This place means more to you than me. My father was right." He shot past her and made it to the rental car he'd barely used since he'd arrived. He hadn't needed it since they'd done everything together.

"The farm is yours as much as mine. We fixed it up together." She threw herself in front of the door to keep him from opening it. "Look at what we've done. Your nana would be so proud of you. She'd be so happy to know you'd returned. It had been what she prayed for most over the years, for your heart to heal and you to find happiness at the farm."

"Temporary stopover, that's all."

She saw his throat bob up and down with a deep swallow.

"Don't do this. Don't walk away again." Juniper broke down into a sob.

He pulled her into his arms, and she thought she'd broken through. His lips pressed to the top of her head and she fell into the comfort and hope and love he had to offer.

"Stay," she managed between heaves.

His entire body stiffened. He shooed her from the door, opened it and climbed inside. "You don't beat my father. You only delay the inevitable. The deed is yours. I'll sign over all rights to you. Go to Gracie. Get those grants and use the money I set up in a trust. Make your program the best in the Southeast and don't waste another thought on me. I'm not worth it." He slammed the door on their conversation and their love.

Rocks spit up from the tires along with dust and doubt. "Don't ever come back here again," she screamed.

"Mommy?" Gracie's little voice sounded from the porch. She stood with tears in her eyes, clutching a bear in one hand and a horse in the other. And despite Juniper's broken heart she swiped her own tears away, knowing she had to be strong for Gracie. At least until she was tucked in bed at night and Juniper could cry alone.

And cry she did, night after night, for over a month. Until she had no more tears to shed.

Chapter Fifteen

Daylight hadn't been in Hudson's life in months. He'd arrive at work before dawn and leave well after midnight. He hated returning to his fancy apartment. Funny how in a city of millions of New Yorkers, he could feel lonelier than on a farm in the middle of nowhere with only two other people.

He collapsed into his desk chair, tossed his laptop bag on the floor and opened his machine to look at the Tetris of appointments shuffled around by his secretary. All that work for one person. His father planned on working him to death before he could think of a way out of his life.

Mark entered Hudson's office and planted himself in the chair facing him. He looked good. His hair had grown back, and he had a love-of-life kind of glow about him. Apparently, surviving cancer did that to a person. "Tonight's the gala. Who you taking?"

The question lingered in the air for a moment, but the only person Hudson could imagine in a pretty dress by his side was Juniper. Wasn't time supposed to heal all wounds? Apparently, a month wasn't long enough. "No time. I need to work on these figures before tomorrow."

"I thought selling our company and getting rich off it while keeping our foot in the door was every man's dream to work less and enjoy life more. That's what you said anyway. When you tried to convince yourself you were doing the right thing. Where's your joy, man?"

Joy. That wasn't a word in Hudson's vocabulary. Not anymore. Maybe if he called Juniper and told her how much he missed her, she'd move here. No, he wouldn't do that to her. She belonged in Willow Oaks, not in this city with skyscrapers strangling the streets, with cars that honked, with people screaming instead of with the cheerful cricket chirps and frogs croaking. Nature's song. How he missed those sounds. "Father has me taking over more so that he can move on to other world-domination projects." The term *father* felt bitter on his tongue.

"Right. And you mourning the loss of your childhood June Bug isn't what has you moping around, yelling at secretaries and scaring delivery people?"

Hudson sighed and dropped his head to his

hands, his elbows resting on his glass desk. "Have I been that bad?"

"The worst." Mark jumped up and smacked the glass surface. "I'm your friend, so I'm going to shoot straight. Either get out and start living life or admit you were wrong and return to the farm."

Hudson's stomach churned. He slid his chair back and dropped his hands to his lap. "Honestly, I don't feel like going out. I'm a minion. That's my one purpose in life."

"No, you're my son, which means you'll be by my side tonight." His father's voice boomed.

Mark had gone along with the sale of their company to his father because he wanted less work and more time for life, but Hudson couldn't help but feel bad that Mark would end up reporting to his father for three years, as laid out in the contract. Three years would be an eternity.

Hudson glowered down at his computer, realizing his father owned him as much as he owned the rest of the world. If this last month had taught Hudson anything, his father didn't care about much other than golf, sports cars and the next big deal. The more he watched his father, the more he realized he didn't want to be like him. "I've got to finish this tonight, so I won't have time to attend."

"Your friend here volunteers to finish. You have a date with a beautiful young woman." His father's brow twitched the way it did when he was nervous or anxious or plotting something big.

"What deal's in trouble?" Hudson asked, out of morbid curiosity, not because he cared about helping. He'd lost all interest in the corporate takeover game.

Father cleared his throat and straightened his tie. "Don't worry yourself about that. I have a plan."

"I don't want to be a part of any more—"

"This has nothing to do with you." His father left in a flash, the same way he'd entered.

Mark sighed. "Great, now you're stuck going and I'm stuck working."

"You could've said no," Hudson said.

"No way. That man scares me. In this city, you don't cross him."

"Not in any city. Not anywhere."

Mark scooted his chair up and settled in to work by Hudson's side, and before they even realized it, the day had come to an end. Together, they managed to finish the proposal, and Mark fled before the old man could give him something else to do.

Hudson spotted the unopened mail from the morning with a letter addressed to him from Willow Oaks. His heart beat fast and energy shot through him. He hadn't felt this kind of excitement since leaving the farm.

No name, only the city, state and zip on the return. His fingers trembled and he said a silent prayer that it was from Juniper even if it wouldn't change anything. One word, even written, would soothe his misery.

Inside, he opened a single sheet of paper that had a flyer for the grand opening of Nana's Hippotherapy and Horse Park. A dried purple flower fell onto his lap as if Gracie had picked it just for him.

His chest burned and he heaved. Tears stung his eyes, but he swiped them away before his father caught him. Even if the man didn't scare him the way he used to, he still controlled the fate of the farm and he wouldn't do anything to jeopardize Juniper and Gracie.

He unlocked the safe he'd installed in the cabinet behind him and pulled out the financial statements he'd managed to acquire for Kenmore Enterprises for the last six months and a land map and paperwork on Willow Oaks.

He eyed his offensive strategy to look for loopholes in his agreement with his father to protect Juniper and Gracie from him doing something underhanded. The shady budgets indicated there was something going on, but it would take a forensic accountant to catch the exact meaning. Part of him guessed his father had overextended some investments, relying on two big ones that took a hit after a natural disaster and a work strike. Still, there was nothing illegal about it that he could tell. He'd keep looking for real ammo, though. He studied the documents one more time and then placed them back into the safe.

With a heavy heart, he folded the paper and placed the flower in his handkerchief to carry in his pocket. He changed into the tux his secretary had arranged to be sent to the office and headed to the car waiting for him downstairs.

His father eyed his watch. "You're late."

"I had to change. What woman have you lined up to be on my arm tonight?" Hudson asked wearily.

"You know, most men are envious of your life. Why do you look so miserable?" Father's words sounded a little less angry or domineering.

"Because I'm not living the life I want." Knowing the land around them had been secured and he had his father's promise not to go after Juniper and the farm, he believed he had nothing to lose, so he opened his mouth. "I'm living the life you wanted. As much as you felt suffocated and trapped on that farm, I feel that now. This city is choking me with its faux friends and backhanded deals. I long for the fresh air and the sunshine and for the touch of a gentle but strong woman, to hold a child and work the land. I'm living your life, not mine. And there's nothing worse than feeling like an impostor in your own life."

The limo pulled up in front of the museum apparently hosting this evening's gala, so Hudson bolted out to find air beyond the stale cigar and whiskey odor of the limo. The coolness of the fall tickled his nostrils, and he imagined the trees were starting to change back in Georgia. It wouldn't be long before they'd be harvesting. Juniper would be taking Gracie to the festival, and they'd probably sell canned preserves the way Nana used to.

Hudson had been so lost in his thoughts he didn't even realize his father and two women had joined him just inside the entrance. The woman's hand slid into his arm. The cameras flashed. People spoke and danced and negotiated deals until Hudson couldn't take it a second longer, but he had no choice. For Juniper and Gracie, he'd put on a tie and work each day if for no other reason than for them to be safe and happy, because he loved them with all his heart from a distance.

The sun rose and set each day, so Juniper knew the world continued to run, but she felt nothing. Numbness didn't begin to explain her emotions. It had taken all her energy to get out of bed, to feed and dress Gracie and face the work and chores in front of her.

Maybe she should've considered going with Hudson when he'd asked. But one glance at Nana's Bible and she knew she'd chosen the right path for herself and Gracie. It didn't make it any easier, though. Sometimes doing the right thing didn't feel good.

She glanced at Gracie holding tight to the old stuffed horse Hudson had given her and offered a fake smile, but Gracie only coiled into herself more.

Papers littered the table. She picked up Nana's Bible that Hudson had left behind and held it to her chest. "God, give me strength," she whispered at the world outside. "My daughter regresses and my heart aches more than I thought it could and still function. I try to move forward but I feel tethered to the past. How do I break free?"

The neigh of the horses outside drew her attention from her self-pity and the journey ahead. Gracie crawled up into her lap and pointed out the window. She'd gone back into her own world and wasn't speaking again, but her eyes glinted each time she looked out the window at the two horses they'd been able to secure. The most gentle and experienced ones they could find, which came with a hefty price tag.

But if the grand opening fundraiser brought in what Juniper hoped, they would be set well into the next year with the grant money promised. At the moment, it appeared Nana's Hippotherapy and Horse Park would remain in the black for the rest of the year.

Two cars pulled up, and a tap of excitement made her heart beat a little more normally. "The therapist is here and so are the helpers. You ready to meet them? You already know one of them."

Gracie shook her head, her braids smacking Juniper in the face. She tugged them and tickled Gracie's belly, eliciting a giggle. With the distraction in place, she swung her into the air and opened the front door to plant her outside to meet the new people.

Gracie snuggled into her side and held tight to her thigh with a cry to go back inside, but it had been a month and they'd mourned long enough for a man who didn't want to be in their lives, or at least couldn't have enough faith to stay and face his father by their side.

A sting shot through her like a wild wasp had been trapped under her skin, but she shoved the thought out of the way and waved Jolene Pearl, the new physical therapist, over along with Mindi, and a new guy, Austin Wilks.

"I'm so excited to have you here." Juniper forced a brilliant smile.

The tall blonde with thin legs, who appeared more like a runway model than a horse whisperer for children, took the stairs two at a time and offered her hand. "Hi, there. Love this place. Of course, I knew I would."

Mindi ran up and flung her arms around Juniper and squealed. "Thanks for hiring me. This'll work great with my new school schedule."

"You did it, then?"

Mindi nodded. "We'll talk more later about it. I'll let you and Jolene get to know each other. I'll take Austin to the barn." She skittered away, appearing more excited than Juniper once had been about opening the hippotherapy program.

Jolene knelt. "This must be Gracie."

Gracie curled more into Juniper and rounded her leg to hide behind her.

"No worries, I can get Mindi or Austin to help me brush the new horses and feed them apples. You don't have to help. I'm sure you don't even like horses much."

Gracie shot out the stuffed horse she hadn't released since Hudson left.

"Oh, that looks like an American quarter horse like the ones we'll be feeding."

Gracie's head poked out from behind Juniper. This woman was good.

"You know, I'll tell you all about when I rode a horse across the plains and ran into wolves and snakes. And how that horse didn't even rear up. Nope, horses are more dependable than people. You show them love, and they're yours for life."

Gracie stepped out and Juniper could see her wheels turning. A promise of an unconditional, never-abandon-you kind of love. But did that exist? Maybe a horse could offer more than people could in this life.

"You'll have to ask your mom if you're allowed to come with me to feed the horses some apples."

Gracie bounced on her toes, and Juniper wanted to blurt yes, but this was an opportunity she couldn't pass up. "Use your words."

Gracie frowned and crossed her arms over her chest with her chin down.

"Maybe next time." Jolene winked and gave an approving head nod.

The most amazing relief flooded Juniper that there would be a woman who understood instead of judging Gracie's behaviors and Juniper's parenting skills.

She liked this woman. She'd come highly recommended, but Juniper couldn't understand why she'd want to come work for less money in a far-off little town in Georgia. Her distant eyes told a story, but Juniper wouldn't pry. Her business didn't matter as long as she could do her job and work well with children. Besides, Juniper wouldn't have to ask. Within days the town would know anything and everything about Jolene Pearl.

"I do. I do."

Progress. Juniper would take it. “Yes, but make sure you listen to everything Ms. Pearl says. Horses are amazing but can be dangerous.”

“We’ll go over all the rules so you can help teach other kids how to handle themselves around horses.”

“I teach?” Gracie asked, her brows shooting high.

“Of course. I was told you were going to be my assistant. You and your mom. Unless you’re not up for the job.”

“I up. I up.” Gracie took Jolene’s hand while still clinging to her stuffed horse.

Juniper looked at the sky and mouthed, *Thank You.*

She hoped Gracie would forget about Hudson and find happiness. If only Juniper could do the same. But no matter how hard she worked during the day, the darkness always rushed in at night. Loneliness took hold and she struggled with facing life without Hudson.

It had been long enough. She’d cried too many tears, and she didn’t want to live for something that would never be. Anger nudged its way in, and she wanted to grab hold and use it to hate Hudson because hate made it easier to deal with the pain.

She returned to her paperwork inside. The light reflected off the gold-embossed lettering of Nana's Bible, and she knew anger wouldn't get her anywhere. She had to forgive the man who'd hurt her if she ever wanted to find peace.

She knelt and prayed for forgiveness, for strength, for hope, for Gracie, for a world that had light instead of darkness.

But before she could stop herself, she prayed for Hudson to walk through the door and announce he'd come home for good.

With a quick glance at the door to confirm that wasn't going to happen, she opened her computer and checked on the outstanding grant proposals she'd submitted. A message popped up with the subject, You Should See This. It was from Mr. Arthur Kenmore. She told herself not to open it, but curiosity won. With one click, she opened the link, and the headline illuminated her screen like a truth beacon.

Billionaire Playboy and Rich, Beautiful Socialite: A Match Made for Media Frenzy

The picture below it was of a dashing Hudson dressed in a tuxedo with a woman on his arm. A stunning and obviously powerful woman. The article deemed them a perfect match.

Her heart cracked and shattered into a zillion pieces, and she thought she'd never be able to put it back together again, but no tears came. She closed her laptop and eyed the Bible. "Thank

You for the answer to my prayers. It might not be what I wanted, but I have closure. I know there is no way I'll ever be able to compete with the life Hudson wants. And that's okay. I'm okay. And Gracie will be okay."

She wasn't sure if she said the words aloud to thank God or reassure herself that she would survive without Hudson. The man she'd loved since she was a child. But she'd have to survive for Gracie.

Chapter Sixteen

His father unceremoniously strutted into Hudson's office and sat down in the leather wingback chair in the corner. "You did well last night. I'm proud of you, son."

For the briefest of moments, pride slithered in, but it triggered an alarm that jolted him with suspicion. "For what?"

He slid his phone from his pocket and airdropped something to Hudson's. "This one night might have sealed the Warnock deal."

He eyed his device and saw a link appear. His pulse tip-tapped up his neck in warning, but he had to know what would make his father proud of him. He opened the article and there it was, an article, a lie. A lie about how he'd claimed to have a future with the heir to the Warnock company.

"Play this right, and we'll be the biggest company in the world." Indeed, pride did shine in his father's eyes, for himself, for being the orchestrator of this deal.

The tip-tap turned to stomping, and his heart joined the beat. "No."

"What?" His father's smile faded, leaving behind a grimace. The kind that signaled the wrath of a powerful man. A man that not only had a heavy hand but a heavy strike in business. Fear reared its ugly head.

Hudson fought to punch it down. Visions of running away from an enraged father, hiding in the hayloft, his nana protecting him from another night of being told how worthless he was and how if he didn't behave more like his father than his mother, he'd die destitute and alone like his mother had.

He'd already lost one woman to his father's abandonment. Did he want to lose another to his own? Because that was what he'd done. The one thing he'd vowed he would never do. He'd abandoned Juniper and Gracie. He was his father. "I said no."

"No to what?"

Hudson saw the way the woman looked at him in the picture on the small screen, with only a "for now" in her eyes. That wasn't how Juniper looked at him. She had looked at him with forever in her eyes, and he'd thrown that aside to save her. Or was it more than that? Had she been right? Was he too scared to stand up to his father? No, he saw it now. "You're right, I'm just like you."

His father's bleached-teeth smile wavered.

"You bury yourself in business, so you never have to feel anything again. It wasn't Mother that never recovered from the loss of your child. It was you." Hudson saw it, the real reason he'd left Juniper and Gracie. His desire never to feel the pain of losing another person in his life the way he'd lost his mother. If he'd turned his father against them, they could lose so much, and what if he couldn't save Juniper the way he'd failed his own mother? Yet, he couldn't live this life another minute. Fear had ruled his actions too long, and he needed to take control.

"Don't be absurd. You're only lashing out because you think you deserve it all. The family and the money. News flash, no one gets everything."

"I won't be your pawn to seal another big deal."

His father shooed off the notion with his over-tanned hand. "Don't be dramatic. There won't be a wedding or anything. Well, not now anyway. I know you still need to sow some wild oats like your old man."

"No, I won't be you anymore. I'm leaving. I quit this job, this life, and I quit running away from what I want because I'm too scared that I'll lose it."

His father's mouth dropped open and his eyes went wide. "You don't mean that."

"I do, and there's nothing you can say to change my mind."

"Where are you going to go? I own fifty-one percent of your company now. You'll have nothing if you leave." He huffed and sat back, snugging his perfectly ironed sleeves a quarter of an inch out of his jacket to show off his expensive cufflinks. "And you won't go back to that farm. We had a deal."

"I'm breaking it. The way you break your promises every day." Hudson rounded his desk. Fear flooded him for the briefest of seconds when his father stood, fists at his side, but it drained from him faster than a sinking dinghy in a storm. "I'll return to the farm, and I don't care about the old company. I have enough money."

"There's never enough." His father laughed heartily, but his eyebrow twitched.

Hudson sensed more to the story. The desperation that flashed in his father's tone. "Are you in financial trouble?"

His father gripped the back of the chair, his nails digging into the leather leaving half-crescent moon indentions when he let go and paced the oversize office. "No. But you're not going anywhere."

"You need me, don't you?" Hudson's anger and resentment and fear all wobbled and tumbled over. "The budgets—the company really is hemorrhaging into debt and you need the Warnock deal, don't you?"

His father's shoulders slumped. "How?"

For the first time in their father-son relationship, Hudson had the upper hand, and he'd need to strike fast before his father recovered. "I'll tell you what. You don't need to answer that, and I'll even make you one last deal."

"What's that?" His father couldn't face him, so he stared out the large picture windows overlooking Manhattan.

"I'll draw up papers stating that you have no rights to the farm and that you relinquish all claims to anything inherited by Juniper Keller from Nana," Hudson said.

His father remained still, hands on hips. Not a word from him, only the noise of people bustling around in the main hall and horns honking outside. Finally, he spoke. "And in exchange, you'll remain here for the rest of this week and dine with Anita Warnock, her father and me for our final deal." His words were sharp and short.

Hudson wouldn't lead the woman on, but something told him she wanted the attention more than the relationship, though he'd make sure to speak with her beforehand. "Done."

His father turned with a defeated expression. "I guess I need to face it."

"What's that?" Hudson asked.

"You're never going to be like me. I tried to give you the best of everything, mold you into a man to be in charge of others and rule the world, but I see it now."

"See what?" Hudson lifted his chin, waiting for his father's next move to slide in and take down the deal in some slimy way.

"That you only want a simple life. It breaks my heart, but if that's what you want, all I've ever wanted was for you to have more than I did growing up. I never wanted you to worry about putting a meal on the table or keeping the electricity on, or losing… Anyway…"

"That's where you're wrong, Father. I have money, and now, with modern technology, I can work from anywhere. I don't have to struggle the way you did. I've got a plan and I hope Juniper will like it, if she'll ever speak to me again."

"Oh, she'll take you back. I saw the way she looked at you when I went to Willow Oaks. Those were the eyes your mother had for me." For the briefest of moments, his voice dipped along with his eyes. There were regrets in his gaze, but less than a second later, he popped back into his blank and emotionless affect and rigid posture.

"I'll have the papers drawn up," his father said.

Hudson offered his hand. "No, I'll have them drawn up and we'll sign them before attending the meeting."

His father took his hand and offered a curt nod. "Looks like you learned something from your old man." He marched out of the office.

In only days, Hudson would be able to see Juniper again. If she'd even speak to him. He'd do anything to make things right. His heart and mind were already on that plane back to Georgia, but first, he needed those papers signed and a plan to win her back. To show her he'd never run again from either of them, no matter what.

He picked up the flyer and held the dried flower between his fingers, and an idea popped into his head. There would be only one way to show he'd be staying permanently. He needed to get to work, and he needed help.

Mindi ushered their best horse, which Gracie had named Flying Squirrel, out of the stall. "That crowd out there is something else. Reminds me of that old movie where they had that stadium and the guy said, 'If you build it, they will come.'"

"*Field of Dreams*. I love that movie." Juniper smiled, and today it didn't take as much energy to fake it, so by tomorrow, she hoped she'd offer one truly genuine.

"I don't think you'll have any trouble financially. Jolene told me someone dropped off a huge check at the donation table that'll keep us afloat for well over a year."

Juniper's heart skidded and skipped. A large donation? She shook off the thought that Hudson had returned. Even if he had something to do with the money, he'd done it from afar. "Who made the donation?"

"Don't know." Mindi shrugged. "Jolene said some man walked up with an envelope and handed it to her. You never know what the future holds, right?"

Juniper shook off her wayward hope that Hudson would strut in on a white horse and declare his love and dedication to this place. And she didn't want to talk about it either. "Something going on with you and the pastor?" Juniper asked. Mindi hadn't been herself the last few days, but they'd been so busy she hadn't had a chance to ask her about it.

"No. We aren't seeing each other. I've got my hands full with my brothers and sisters, and it's a lot to take on with school. Ready for the main event?"

"Hopefully the grand finale will be evidence of our work here." They were to walk the corral to showcase Gracie's progress. And Gracie had made progress over the last month or so. The horses and the therapist had done more for Gracie than Juniper had managed in the last year.

Part of her wanted to be upset for being a failure as a mother, but she was done with those thoughts. No more allowing the judgment of others to pollute her self-confidence. James had done that for too long, and she wouldn't allow another person to have that kind of control over her.

Gracie skipped into the barn in a princess costume, holding Jolene's hand. Gracie wanted to make a real appearance, and Jolene said it would be good for the show and would bring in even more donations. The woman knew her way around horses and hippotherapy. Juniper only hoped she'd want to stay awhile.

"I'll go get ready to make the announcements." Mindi raced out of the barn.

Jolene looked out the side window. "What's Ace Gatlin's deal? He's got a limp, but when I tried to speak with him about it, he shut me down and ushered me out of the feedstore."

"War. Came back with scars beyond those we can see. He almost stopped this all from happening. I'm not sure why, but Nana said bitterness breeds poor deeds."

"Gotcha." She patted Flying Squirrel and took Gracie to the other side—careful to walk around the front as she reminded her about the rules—and helped her up into the saddle. Juniper took her position on one side and Jolene stood on the other. Juniper carefully positioned her arm in the place Jolene had shown her, and they walked to the barn doors and waited.

Mindi repeated how the donations would be used for the program, but in the middle, she cut off, and Juniper couldn't hear anything.

"Oh no, the mic must've stopped working," she said to Jolene.

Jolene chuckled. "Something always has to go wrong with these kinds of events. If that's all, don't worry. I'm sure Mindi can project to the crowd. I've heard her sing in church."

The barn doors slid open, and they walked Flying Squirrel and Gracie outside so all could see her perform on the horse after they'd seen the video of her initial session. Wow, had she come a long way in confidence, speech, balance and temperament.

The cool, brisk autumn air rustled the banners lining the fence, and the people applauded but then fell silent.

"Hud. Hud!" Gracie squealed.

Juniper snapped her attention to Gracie, unsure what to say. She'd explained to her so many times that he wasn't going to return, but she still called out to him at least once a day.

"Hud. Hud!" Gracie pointed, and Juniper's eyes followed her finger to the end. And across the corral stood Hudson Kenmore in jeans, a button-up and boots, holding purple wildflowers in one hand along with the microphone in the other.

Juniper's legs stopped, and so did the horse's.

"Is this part of the performance?" Jolene asked.

"Hud, Hud…" Gracie squirmed, but Jolene reminded her to remain on the horse until they were done. Mindi ran over as if she'd been in on some secret and nudged into Juniper's position by Gracie's side.

"Many of you know that I grew up in Willow Oaks and that my father was a controlling man." Hudson's voice echoed through the corral, the fields, the world. Juniper's world.

Grumbles rolled through the crowd.

"You also know that I lost my mother at a young age, and my nana and this woman, Juniper Keller, were all I had left in this world. But I couldn't do it. I couldn't open my heart fully to them because I didn't want to face losing another person that I cared about. You see, it was easier to remain closed off to love than to feel such pain again. I didn't realize it until I discovered the truth about my own father. My parents lost a daughter when I was four years old because my father was too poor to take care of the family the way he wanted to. That's why he's spent his life making money. He pushed my mother out of his life to protect his heart. And I don't want to make the same mistakes he did."

Juniper shuffled toward him, blinking as if to see more clearly, because Hudson couldn't be here. Maybe he'd come for the day to show his support, but he'd leave tomorrow. But she didn't want him here for only one day. It would complicate things further for Gracie.

"Love can be torturous and beautiful. Love can be complicated and simple. Love can be lonely and wonderful. It took me a long time to realize I pushed people away, despite a smart, dedicated, amazing, beautiful and talented woman warning me I'd find myself alone someday."

The crowd *aww*ed.

"I'm afraid that my fear led me to make some cowardly decisions. First, when I graduated high school, my father told me to go to college and leave the farm, and when I said I wouldn't, he threatened to take the farm away from Nana. I told myself his threat was what made me leave, but it wasn't. For a second time, only a couple of months ago, my father threatened to shut this place down, so I told myself I left to protect Juniper and Gracie, but I left to protect myself. Only I discovered something."

"What?" Ace shouted.

Juniper moved closer, her breath caught between her lungs and hope, but she couldn't go there. She'd send him away.

"I only found loneliness, just like Nana had warned me. A loneliness that carves out a piece of you and leaves you feeling empty inside. But then I realized something."

Juniper found her shaky voice and asked, "What?" Her throat constricted as if to tell her not to speak. The pounding in her ears roared so loudly she thought her body protected her from listening.

"I realized that a moment of having Juniper and Gracie Keller in my life, even if I was to lose them tomorrow and live in sorrow the rest of my days, was better than one second wasted not being with them while God granted me this gift." He held out the flowers to Juniper, but she didn't take them. She couldn't. She couldn't believe Hudson Kenmore would want to stay here.

"We've been through this. I can't leave, and you can't stay. There is not, and never will be, an us." Tears stung her eyes, but she cleared her throat and raised her chin.

The crowd had gone silent. Only the sound of Flying Squirrel's hoofs against the hard-packed ground echoed through the corral as Gracie approached on the horse.

Hudson handed over the flowers to Gracie, gave her a quick kiss, and then pulled something out of his pocket. "That's where you're wrong." He lowered to one knee and opened the little black box to a mountainous rock resting on a circle of silver. "I, Hudson Kenmore, wish to live here for the rest of my days, to work the land by your side, and to love you until my last breath, because, Juniper Keller, I love you. You've shown me how to let God back into my heart, how I could be a good father to a special little girl, and how to love again. Juniper, I never want to leave my home again. Can I stay and be a father to Gracie and a husband to you? Will you marry me?"

Sniffles and *aww*s broke through her pounding pulse.

Her mouth went dry, palms sweaty. Jolene must've dismounted Gracie, because she ran over and threw herself into Hudson's arms. He squeezed her tight and kissed her forehead.

"I—I..." Juniper's chest ached, and she wanted to join them, to be in their arms and to live together as a family, but how could she believe his words again?

She looked up to the sky for a sign—any indication that this would be the right decision in her life. With eyes closed, she said a silent prayer asking for guidance, and a peace coated the roaring anxiety into a simmer of concern.

Gracie threw her arms around Juniper. "Nana told me."

Juniper blinked at her little girl. "Told you what, sweetheart?"

"Dream. She say Hud be my daddy."

"You had a dream with Nana in it, and she told you Hudson and I would get married?"

"Uh-huh. Uh-huh." Gracie fisted her hands

near her shoulders and shook with excitement. "Said we family."

Tears streamed down Juniper's face, and she shook so hard Hudson ran to help her up. "Will you?"

"Answer the poor man," Mr. Chester shouted.

Juniper swallowed down her bitterness and worry and allowed the love to pour over her. "Yes, I'll marry you."

Hudson pulled her into a tight embrace and kissed her. Kissed her with passion, love and promise. A promise he'd never leave her again.

* * * * *

Dear Reader,

This story was born from the gracious gift God gave me in a child who was challenged with PDD-NOS. In his early years, he struggled to connect with the world around him, often overlooked or dismissed, just as I was with my own unique challenges as a child. Yet, he has grown into a well-educated, handsome young man, showing no trace of his former challenges—a true testament to the potential within every child.

I'm thankful to Love Inspired for the chance to shine a light on children like Gracie, providing an opportunity to bring clarity and education about the extraordinary gifts these little ones offer our world. Many are affectionate, passionate and full of grace, capable of blessing our hearts with their kindness. Each milestone Gracie achieved brought tears to my eyes, knowing the tremendous effort she put into each daily task, reminding us to always have faith and never give up. She is the true heroine of this story, bringing two lost loves back together with a little help from Hudson's late grandmother.

Almost all of my fifty-plus "Southern Grace to Western Embrace" romance stories feature characters with challenges inspired by my former work with special needs individuals and my personal experiences. You can read about my journey from being labeled as mentally retarded as a child to becoming a USA Today bestselling author, as well as explore all my books, at ciaraknight.com.

Blessings,
Ciara Knight